"Tess, we need to talk."

Nick sat on the edge of Tess's bed. "Why can't we just get along?"

Tess shut her eyes so she wouldn't be tempted to kiss him. "Because if we get along, I'll end up sleeping with you."

Nick shot her an outraged look. "You start fights so we won't have sex?"

"Not always. Sometimes you're such a yuppie I *have* to fight with you. But a lot of the time, yes."

Tess waited for Nick to leave in disgust. The disappointment that thought engendered made her weak. She didn't want him to leave. Maybe it was time to stop saying no. Maybe—

Think of something else, she commanded herself. Then she looked at Nick and knew that she wasn't going to think of anything else. So she pulled him down and kissed him.

Jennifer Crusie lives in a small Ohio town with four cats, three dogs, two mortgages and a teenager. She began reading romances for a university research project—and enjoyed them so much, she decided to try writing one. She not only *tried* but has succeeded! *Strange Bedpersons* is Jennifer's fourth published book.

STRANGE BEDPERSONS

JENNIFER CRUSIE

Harlequin Books

TORONTO • NEW YORK • LONDON
AMSTERDAM • PARIS • SYDNEY • HAMBURG
STOCKHOLM • ATHENS • TOKYO • MILAN
MADRID • WARSAW • BUDAPEST • AUCKLAND

This book is for Eric Walborn
1960-1993
Because there was no one in the world like Eric,
So bright, so kind, so loving, so full of life,
So apt to make jokes and to understand them,
Also his face was beautiful, and we loved him.

ISBN 0-373-25620-5

STRANGE BEDPERSONS

Copyright © 1994 by Jennifer Crusie.

All rights reserved. Except for use in any review, the reproduction or
utilization of this work in whole or in part in any form by any electronic,
mechanical or other means, now known or hereafter invented, including
xerography, photocopying and recording, or in any information storage
or retrieval system, is forbidden without the written permission of the
publisher, Harlequin Enterprises Limited, 225 Duncan Mill Road,
Don Mills, Ontario, Canada M3B 3K9.

All characters in this book have no existence outside the imagination of
the author and have no relation whatsoever to anyone bearing the same
name or names. They are not even distantly inspired by any individual
known or unknown to the author, and all incidents are pure invention.

This edition published by arrangement with Harlequin Enterprises B.V.

® and TM are trademarks of the publisher. Trademarks indicated with
® are registered in the United States Patent and Trademark Office, the
Canadian Trade Marks Office and in other countries.

Printed in U.S.A.

1

WHEN TESS NEWHART threw open her apartment door, Nick Jamieson was standing there—tall, dark, successful and suspiciously happy to see her, his pleasantly blunt face a nice human contrast to his perfectly tailored suit. She stared at him warily, fighting down the ridiculous jolt of relief and happiness and lust that welled up in her just because he was back.

Then he threw his arms wide to hug her.

"Tess!" he said, beaming at her. "You look great!"

Tess looked down at her sagging, bleach-splotched sweatshirt and faded blue sweatpants, the hems shrunk to midcalf on her long legs. So much for relief, happiness and lust. She rolled her eyes at him, all her suspicions confirmed. "Right." She slammed the door in his face and shot home both dead bolts.

"Aw, come on, Tess," Nick called through the door. "It's been a month. Actually it's been a month, a week and two days, but who's counting? All right, I'm counting. I miss you. I keep calling but you won't call me back. Is that fair? I think we should talk about this."

"I don't," Tess said firmly to the door, but her face was uncertain as she ran her fingers through her short red curls. If Nick hadn't had such a large streak of calculating rat running through him, he would have been just what she needed at the moment, instead of the last thing she needed. But there was that streak of rat, and if he was at her door being charming it was because he wanted something. And the something probably wasn't her. It was something to do with money, promotion, status or all of the above. She shook her head, newly determined, and turned back to cross the threadbare gray carpeting to her chair and her conversation.

"Who's the wise guy? Your landlord?" Gina DeCosta sprawled on Tess's lumpy couch, a symphony in black: her unruly black hair falling into her eyes, her small body lost in a huge black T-shirt, and her legs wrapped in black leggings as tight as Ace bandages. She stretched out those legs tentatively and winced.

"Worse." Tess flopped down into her decrepit armchair, which groaned under her weight, and slung her long legs over the side. "You know, every time I think my life has hit bottom, somebody lowers the bottom."

Nick pounded on the door. "Come on, Tess. Open up."

"Who *is* that guy?" Gina said.

"Nick, but I don't want to talk about it," Tess said, forestalling Gina before she could leap into the breach. "Between him and my landlord, I may never open that door again." Tess patted her lap, and a huge black cat jumped into her arms, reclaiming the territory she'd lost when Tess had gone to answer the door. "Sorry, Angela," Tess murmured to the cat.

"Tess?" Nick called. "Come on. Let's be adult about this. Or you can be adult and I'll fake it. Tess?"

Gina frowned at the door. "Why are you ducking Nick?"

"Well," Tess said, and thought for a minute. "It's like this." She stood up, dumping the cat off her lap again. "I answered the door and he said—" she flung her arms wide and beamed a toothpaste smile at Gina "—Tess, you look *great!*"

Gina looked at Tess's sweats. "Uh-oh."

"Exactly." Tess flopped back into her chair. "You know, every time I see Nick, my mind looks at him and says, 'Yes, he's fun, but he's also a power-hungry rat, so stay away from him,' and then my body looks at him and says, 'Hello, gorgeous, come to Mama.'" She shook her head. "I have to have a long talk with my body."

Gina looked at the sweats again. "I don't think it's gonna listen to you. If you dressed me like that, *I* wouldn't listen to you."

"Forget the clothes," Tess said. "You're starting to sound like Nick."

"Okay. New topic. Why are you waiting for your landlord?"

"I reported him to the housing commission." Tess smiled, visibly cheered up by the thought.

"Well, that was unfriendly," Gina said. "What did he do?"

"It's what he didn't do." Tess shifted in her chair as she warmed to the story of her landlord's crimes. "Three apartments in this building have been vandalized in the past two months, and Ray won't even fix the lock on the hall door. Anybody can walk in here. Somebody had to do something." She grinned at Gina. "And, I thought, who better than me?"

"Tess?" Nick called again. "It's not safe out here. If I get mugged because you're playing hard to get, you'll never forgive yourself."

Both women turned to look at the door, and then Gina looked at Tess. Tess shrugged.

"Okay," Gina said, abandoning the subject of Nick. "So you did something. That's no big surprise. I'm just amazed you did something as calm as reporting him."

"Well, I thought about organizing a candlelight-vigil protest march," Tess said, starting to grin again. "I thought all the tenants could light candles and march on Ray's condominium, but this place is such a firetrap I knew we'd never make it to the front door alive, so then I thought about using

Bic lighters, instead, but that made me think of Stanley across the hall."

"Stanley?"

"You've never seen Stanley?" Tess's grin widened. "Stanley always wears the same T-shirt and it doesn't cover his tummy, and Stanley's tummy is not attractive. In fact . . ." Tess's face took on a faraway look. "In fact, Stanley's stomach is the only one I've ever seen with a five-o'clock shadow." She frowned at Gina. "Do you suppose he shaves it?"

Gina made a face. "That's gross."

"I think so, too, which is why I couldn't picture Stanley with a Bic. A torch, yes. A Bic, no." Tess smiled again. "But then I thought, why not give Stanley a pitchfork and put him at the head of the march?" She stopped to visualize it. "You know, there's a lot of Quasimodo in Stanley."

"Come on, Tess, cut me a break here," Nick called. "I came back to apologize. Doesn't that count for something?"

Gina raised an inquiring eyebrow at Tess, but Tess shook her head, so Gina returned to Stanley and the pitchfork. "I don't think Quasimodo had a pitchfork," she said. "He didn't in the movie."

"Anyway, I finally had to get serious before somebody around here got hurt," Tess said. "So I acted like an adult and filed the report."

"Good choice," Gina said. "Getting arrested for pitchforking Stanley would probably have been bad for your career."

"Well, actually my career is sort of dead right now." Tess slumped down in her chair. "I wasn't going to tell you since this is your first night back from the tour and I was looking forward to one night without trauma, but . . . I lost my job."

"Oh, no." Gina sat up, her face bleak with sympathy and concern. "What happened?"

"Don't panic," Tess said from the depths of her chair. "I have a plan."

"Sure you do," Gina said. "What happened?"

"Funding cuts. The education governor we elected decided that supporting private-tutoring foundations wasn't educational. So now the Foundation is going to have to only use volunteers. Eventually the whole place may go."

"Tess, I'm really sorry," Gina said. "Really. I know how much those kids meant to you."

"Hey." Tess straightened and glared at Gina with mock severity. "I'm not finished yet. The kids aren't leaving. And neither am I. I just have to find a job to pay my bills that gives me my afternoons free so I can still volunteer there." She grinned. "I saw *Pretty Woman* the other night on TV, and Julia Roberts was having such a good time being objectified by Richard Gere that I seriously thought about taking up hooking, but then I thought, thirty-six is a little old to hit the streets."

Nick knocked again. "Tess? You want me to grovel? I'll grovel. I've got a great grovel. You've never seen my grovel—you left before I could show it to you. Come on, Tess, let me in."

Gina jerked her head toward the door. "If you're thinking about swapping your bod for money, go answer the door. He's still loaded, right?"

Tess nodded. "I haven't checked lately, but knowing Nick and his affinity for money, he's still loaded."

"Marry him," Gina said.

"No," Tess said.

"Why not?"

"Well, to begin with, he hasn't asked me," Tess answered. "And he's a Republican lawyer, so my mother would disown me. And then—" Tess frowned "—I always thought it would be a good idea to marry somebody who wouldn't try to pick up the maid of honor at the reception. Call me crazy but—"

"Since that would be me, you got no worries. Marry him."

"You don't know Nick," Tess said. "He could seduce Mother Teresa." She cocked her head toward the door and listened for a moment. "And it doesn't seem to be an option anymore. I think he got tired and left." She tried hard not to be disappointed. After all, she'd had no intention of opening the door anyway.

Still, it wasn't like Nick to give up that fast, dangerous hallway or not. He must not have missed her that much, after all.

Damn.

NICK LEANED against the wall outside Tess's door and analyzed the situation. Pounding was obviously not getting him anyplace, and his charm was bombing, too, which was a new experience for him. What the hell was wrong here? Maybe she was still mad, but she couldn't be that mad. Not Tess. Tess erupted all over the place and then forgot about it. She'd never sulked in her life. So there was something else keeping her from falling at his feet. Nick grinned at the thought. Okay, she'd never fallen at his feet. But she'd never slammed a door in his face, either.

She was upset about something.

That wasn't good. He liked Tess, and the thought of her being unhappy bothered him. He spared a fleeting thought of concern for her and then returned to his own problem.

She wasn't upset with him. She hadn't slammed the door on him right away, so it was something else. Probably one of her lame ducks in trouble. And when he'd tried that dumb line about her looking great—when she actually looked like hell—she'd gotten exasperated and slammed the door. All right, so he deserved the door. Now all he had to do was get the door open again, give her a little sympathy, and he'd be in.

If he waited half an hour and then knocked again, she might open it, thinking he'd gone away.

And if he had flowers or candy or something . . . No. Not for Tess. Tess would not be impressed with generic peace offerings. He thought about the problem for another minute and then left, surveying the gloomy hall with contempt as he went.

"I THINK you shoulda let him in," Gina said. "Rich lawyers don't grow on trees." She flexed her right leg cautiously. "Hey, you got any muscle rub? My calves are killing me."

"I don't have time to toy with Nick right now. I have to work on my plan." Tess rose and walked the few steps across her tiny apartment to her bathroom, stepping over several sloppy stacks of books, a pile of mismatched socks, a bundle of partly graded essays and a half-finished poster that said I Read Banned Books. She kept talking as she went, and her voice rose and fell as she went out of and came back into the room. "I have a chance at a teaching job, but I don't know if I can get it. I'm not really qualified for it, and it would be working with a bunch of rich kids, so they'd probably think I was an alien, but the money is good and the hours are great."

She handed Gina the tube of muscle cream and dropped back into her chair.

Gina squirted the cream onto her fingers. "Go for it. It beats starving." She winced as she rubbed the cream into her calf.

Tess sat up, her job problems forgotten. "Are you all right? I thought this was just your usual dancer's cramp."

"No, I'm not all right," Gina said. "I'm thirty-five. I'm not snapping back like I used to." She rubbed her calves again, frowning at the ache. "I'm starting to really hate the pain. I never liked it, but now I'm starting to hate it."

Tess wasn't sure what to say. "How can I help?"

Gina laughed. "You can't. It's age."

"Don't be ridiculous," Tess began, but Gina waved her into silence.

"Honey, I'm the Grandma Moses of the chorus line."

"Don't be ridiculous," Tess said again. "You work all the time. You're never out of a job. How many dancers can say that?"

"I'm never out of a job because I always show up, I'm never sick, I never screw up, and I never leave the show in New Jersey to get married." Gina stretched out her legs, the pain reflected in her face easing a little. "But that's not gonna carry me forever." She shrugged. "'Course, neither will my legs." She stared at them as if they were something she'd picked up on sale and now regretted. "I don't think I ever want to do another plié again."

"You're joking." Tess fell silent for half a second and then regrouped. "What do you want to do?"

"I want to get married," Gina said.

Tess sank back into her chair. "Married? This is new."

"Not really. I always wanted to get married," Gina said wistfully. "I just wanted a career first." She smiled a little. "Big career I got. Now I want some peace and quiet. Some security." She looked at Tess, suddenly vulnerable. "You know, some love. I never found anybody on the road, which is no big surprise when I think about it. But now I'm ready. I want a house and kids and the whole bit."

"Is this because you never got out of the chorus?" Tess said. "Because think about all the people who never got *in* . . ."

"I never wanted out of the chorus." Gina flexed her legs again and winced. "I never wanted to be a star. I never wanted all that attention. I just wanted to be part of the show. And that's what I want now. I don't need some big, important guy.

I just want to find a nice, unimportant guy and be part of his show."

"As a feminist, I should probably say something here," Tess said. "But I won't, because it's your life."

"Thanks," Gina said. "I appreciate that."

"I know some nice guys from the Foundation," Tess said. "Of course they're out of work now, but they're . . ."

Gina shook her head. "I can do this on my own, Tess. Forget about fixing my life." She shot another look around the apartment. "You got your own to fix first, anyway."

"Me? I'm not ready to get married. I never even think about it." Tess looked around the apartment, too. "Well, I hardly ever think about it."

Gina's eyebrows shot up. "Hardly?"

"Well, every now and then I have these fantasies where I wear an apron and say, 'Hi, honey, how was your day?' to somebody gorgeous who immediately makes love to me on the kitchen table."

Gina looked confused. "Sounds like *Betty Crocker Does Dallas*."

"I know." Tess frowned. "I don't think I'm cut out to be a wife. I mean, I get lonely sometimes, and I start thinking about how nice it would be to be a homey sort of person and bake cherry pie for somebody, but then one thing leads to another and I'm having fantasies about somebody ripping off my apron and licking cherry juice off my body, and I lose my grip." She focused back on Gina. "Besides, I can't bake pie. So I don't think about getting married much."

Gina scowled at her. "How could you get lonely? You think it's your job to save everybody in the world. You gotta know more grateful people than—"

"Well, sometimes it would be nice not to save everybody," Tess said. "Sometimes I think it would really be nice to be taken care of and live in a house, instead of an apartment, and to have great sex every night." Tess stopped. "I've got to get off this sex thing. It's clouding my mind. The career, Tess, concentrate on the career." She shook her head. "Now I'm starting to sound like Nick."

"Speaking of Nick, why'd you shut the door on him? That's prime home-building material there."

Tess laughed. "You obviously don't know Nick. The only reason he'd build a home is for the equity. In fact, that's the reason he did build a house." She leaned her head back against the chair, remembering. "The skeleton of the place was up about the time I left him. We walked through it once, and I was trying to figure out what it would look like, and he was trying to figure out how much it would appreciate in value the first year." Tess grinned. "It was not a Kodak moment for us."

"Did you have Kodak moments?"

"Yeah," Tess said, her grin fading. "We did. Quite a few actually." She stood up suddenly and went into her bedroom.

"Tess?" Gina called.

"Here," Tess said when she came back. She sat beside Gina on the edge of the couch and showed her a snapshot. It was Nick, a smudge of dirt on his chin and his hair in his eyes, in an old sweatshirt with the sleeves cut off, sitting on the ground with his arms wrapped around Tess from behind, his chin buried in her shoulder. Tess was even more of a mess: her red hair stood straight up and her face was dirty, and she had no makeup on at all. Her smile took up her whole face, and she looked about ten.

"What were you doing?" Gina asked, mystified.

"This is the first day we met." Tess smiled at the picture. "At a picnic. Playing touch football. He was wearing these really ratty jeans and a sweatshirt that was older than my sweatshirt, and I thought he was poor and cheerful, like the prince in my fairy tale." She laughed. "Boy, was I wrong."

Gina took the picture and looked at Nick more closely. "Even messed up, he's gorgeous, Tess."

"I know," Tess said. "But looks aren't everything. It was those damn crinkles he gets around his eyes when he smiles that threw me off, but he was definitely the wrong prince." She shook her head and sighed. "It wasn't long before I caught on, though. I mean, we were obviously not the perfect couple. We went to this opera thing the night we broke up, and the press took our picture." She grinned at Gina. "Actually the press took Nick's picture and got me because I was standing beside him. It finally made the society page a couple of days ago." Her grin widened as she remembered the picture. "Nick looked like a Kennedy cousin. I looked like a rutabaga with hair. All over Riverbend, people looked at that picture and said, 'What does he see in her?'" Tess shook her head again. "We definitely do not belong together."

Gina handed the photo back. "I still don't get the prince bit."

Tess moved back to her own chair, looking sadly at the print. "Remember I told you I lived in a commune when I was little?" she said, her fingertip stroking the edge of the photo. "Well, my mother wouldn't let me read Cinderella and the other fairy tales. She said they were patriarchal and sexist, and I was really disappointed, so a friend of hers at the commune, this guy named Lanny, made up this story for me that he called CinderTess." She laughed at the sound of it.

"Cute," Gina said. "But I still don't get the prince."

"Well, CinderTess got to the ball on her own without any fairy godmother by rescuing people and animals who turned out to be able to help her," Tess explained. "But she felt responsible for them and their problems, so when she got to the ball, and she was the best dancer there—"

"Not the prettiest?" Gina asked, grinning.

"Looks are superficial. Real women get by on hard work and skill," Tess said primly, and grinned back. "Where was I?"

"She was the best dancer . . ." Gina prompted.

"So while she had all the attention because she was the best, she sort of made speeches about the problems. There was one about the environment and one about the poor, I think. I never really paid attention to those parts and only listened to the good ones—about the prince." She smiled again, remembering. "I didn't care about the politically correct part. I just wanted a fairy tale with a prince."

Gina laughed. "Who doesn't? So where's the prince?"

"There were two of them who got upset about the speeches. But the third prince said she was right and helped her and—this is the part I always liked—he had these crinkles . . ." she screwed up her face to make laugh lines at the corners of her eyes ". . . right here, and he promised her he'd help her make things better and that she'd laugh every day if she married him, so CinderTess knew he was the one." She looked back down at the picture. "I'm sure Lanny meant well, but those crinkles have played merry hell with my life ever since I met Nick."

Someone knocked on the door.

"Must be the landlord," Gina said. "Try not to hurt him too bad."

Tess tossed the snapshot on the end table and stood up, tipping her exasperated cat out of her lap again, but when she opened the door, it was Nick.

"I know you're upset, so I won't bother you for long." He smiled at her, his dark eyes brimming with the confident charm she found alternately obnoxious and irresistible, depending on the reason he was using it on her. There were crinkles at the corners of his eyes, and a lock of his hair fell over one eye and made him look rakish and endearing.

Tess was sure he knew he looked rakish and endearing.

Still, he also knew she was troubled, and that was touching.

His smile broadened as she hesitated. "I brought you something to cheer you up," he said, handing her a carton of Chinese food.

"What is it?" Tess said, taking it from him, knowing she shouldn't but weakening.

"Pot stickers," Nick said. "Double order."

"Oh." Tess blinked at him. "You remembered."

"I remember everything," Nick said, and Tess's uncertain expression turned to contempt.

"That sounds like a line," she said. "Did you really come back to apologize, or is this something that you and that weasel you work for have cooked up to close some deal?"

"Park? Funny you should mention Park—" Nick said, and Tess slammed the door in his face again and went back to her chair, dropping the pot stickers on the table as she sat.

"He's hopeless," Tess began, and then she jumped when Nick opened the door and closed it behind him, throwing the dead bolts.

"Lock your door, dummy," he said. "This is a terrible neighborhood. Anybody could walk in here."

"Anybody just did." Tess put her hands on her hips, faking indignation. "Go away."

Nick headed for the kitchen, stopping only to pat Gina on the head. "Hi, kid. Good to see you again. You look great."

Gina beamed and started to say something, but he'd moved on by then. She checked herself, her smile fading, and then she dug in her purse until she found a stick of gum.

"Excuse me?" Tess called after him. "I did not invite you in."

Nick backtracked swiftly and kissed her. She softened into him for just an instant, giving herself just a second of his warmth before she ripped into him as he so richly deserved. But before she could retaliate he let her go and again headed for her tiny kitchen. "God, this place is a mess," he said. "Is any of my beer still in the fridge?" He stepped over the cat as it made for Tess's lap. "Hello, Angela. Try not to shed on me."

Tess looked at Gina.

"Definitely time to talk to the body," Gina said. "If you'd had an apron on, *you* woulda ripped it off."

Tess jerked on the hem of her sweatshirt and lowered her chin, trying to psych herself into being impressive. "You've been rejected," she called to Nick. "Leave."

"You can't reject a proposal you've never heard," Nick said from the kitchen.

"You're proposing?" Tess said in disbelief. "I don't believe it."

Gina's eyebrows shot up. "Marriage?" she whispered to Tess around her gum. "Grab him."

"Of course not marriage," Tess said to Gina. "What are you proposing?" she asked Nick. "Whatever it is, the answer is no, of course, but I like to know what I'm rejecting."

"Well, not marriage." Nick came to lean in the doorway with his beer, smiling at her, solidly attractive, boyishly confident and infinitely desirable. *Stop it*, Tess told herself, and narrowed her eyes at him.

"I need a date for the weekend," he said, and widened his grin. "I thought of you first."

"Why?" Tess said, trying to stomp on the little sizzle that had started inside her when he smiled at her.

"Because I need you," Nick said. "My life has been empty since you walked out." He twisted the cap off the beer and began to drink.

"Your life has never been empty, even after I walked out."
Tess swung her gaze to Gina. "I picked him up at the airport
one day, and the stewardess kissed him goodbye. You'd have
thought he was going off to war. She did everything but offer to have his baby right there on the spot."

Nick choked on his beer. "She was just a friend," he said,
swallowing. "I'm a friendly guy."

"I realize that," Tess said, crossing her arms. "Get out."

"Tess, honey." Nick leaned forward and smiled at her.
"Sweetie. Baby."

"Boy, you must really be in trouble," Tess said.

"Up to my neck," Nick said. "I need you. One weekend.
No strings."

"No sex," Tess said, ignoring her body. "That offer will not
be repeated."

"Whatever you say," Nick agreed. "If that's the way you
want it, no sex."

Tess turned to Gina. "This must be bad. I think he really
is in trouble."

"So of course you gotta save him." Gina smiled shyly at
Nick. "I'm all for it. For once those do-gooder instincts of hers
are gonna do her some good."

"You know, I always liked you," Nick said to Gina, and she
blushed with pleasure.

"Actually I don't care if I save him or not, but if I go with
him this weekend, I'll get to watch," Tess said. "If it's really
big trouble, I may feel avenged for that war bride of a stewardess."

"You're all heart," Nick said to her.

"Although it won't make up for the night you stood me up
at the Foundation benefit." Tess made a face. "And definitely not for that night you turned me down in the Music
Hall parking lot. I know women who'd be slashing your tires
and poisoning your beer for that night alone."

Nick started and glanced down at the bottle in his hand.

Tess studied him with a sinking heart and rising heat. He was easily the most attractive thing in her apartment. In fact, he was easily the most attractive thing in her life. Of course, looks were superficial. Especially on Nick who had more faces than Sybil.

She cast an uncertain look at Gina, still stretched out on the couch.

Gina cracked her gum. "Do it."

"Maybe." Tess turned back to Nick. "Give me the details. And this better be good."

"It's terrible," Nick said.

Gina swung her legs to the floor, winced and stood up. "This sounds like my exit cue."

"No, it isn't," Tess said at the same time Nick said, "Thank you. You have terrific instincts."

"Hey." Tess said, but Gina picked up her purse.

"I have to be going, anyway," she told Tess. "I love you, but I don't want to hang out in your neighborhood after dark, and I really need more of this muscle stuff on my legs. Call me later and tell me everything."

"You know, that's an intelligent woman," Nick said when she was gone.

"That's the woman you said was wasting her life in tights," Tess reminded him.

Nick winced. "I didn't exactly say that. I said that dancing wasn't much of a career, and she was going to be in trouble someday if she didn't plan ahead."

"Well, some people live for the moment," Tess grumped. She flopped back into her chair and tried to forget that Gina was in trouble right now because she hadn't planned ahead. One of the more annoying things about Nick was that he was often right.

"I was wrong. I'm sorry." Nick opened his mouth to go on, but Tess shook her head.

"Forget it. I'm in a bad mood and I'm taking it out on you. Now, explain this mess to me." She craned her neck to look up at him. "But don't explain it looming over me." She waved him to the floor. "Sit." She watched him slide down the wall beside her chair to sit at her feet, his broad body graceful even in collapse. She grinned at him. "This is good. You understand the basic commands."

"Come down here with me and I'll roll over," Nick said, and Tess felt her pulse flutter.

"Go away," she said.

"Forget I said that," Nick said. "That was my evil twin."

"The only evil twin you have is that twit you work for," Tess said.

"Funny, you should mention Park..." Nick began again.

IT HADN'T SEEMED like a disaster to Nick when he'd walked blithely into his office at Patterson and Patterson a couple of hours earlier. Walking into Patterson and Patterson always made him feel good, anyway. There was something about the ambiance of grossly expensive imported mahogany paneling, grossly expensive imported Oriental carpets, grossly expensive antique furniture and moderately expensive secretarial help at his beck and call that made him feel like a robber baron. And that afternoon, life had been especially good: an important and unexpectedly swift victory in court, a grateful client and an afternoon that was suddenly his to spend any way he wanted. If the lettering on the door had only said Patterson, Patterson and Jamieson, life would have been perfect.

Then things started to go downhill.

"I'm back, Christine," he'd said to his secretary, an unflappable, beautiful brunette in her thirties who'd been totally unimpressed with him since the day he'd hired her.

Christine looked up at him, barely interested.

"No, don't get up," he said on his way into his office. "I can find my way."

Christine drifted to her feet and followed him, giving the impression she'd been going that way, anyway. "Mr. Patterson was in today," she told him. "And Park wants to see you."

"You put that well." Nick shrugged off his jacket and dropped it on a chair. He sat down at his desk, glanced at the framed snapshot on it with an absentminded half smile, and then leaned back in his chair, tugging at his tie. "Park's dad put him in a snit again, but you're too tactful to say that. No wonder we pay you a fortune."

"I need a raise," Christine said without changing her tone or expression. "And I wouldn't call it a snit. More like a catatonic panic."

Nick loosened his tie and sighed a little in relief. "I hate ties. Some woman must have thought them up for revenge." He cocked an eye at Christine. "You wouldn't have had anything to do with that, would you?"

"Yes," Christine said. "You also have several messages from women. None from Tess."

Nick's eyes went to the picture on his desk and then back to Christine. "Why would I want to hear from Tess?"

"Because you keep calling her and she doesn't call back," Christine said with great and obvious patience. "Your messages are on your desk. Park is in his office. Pacing."

Nick ignored the messages. "Anything I should know before I see him?"

"How would I know?" Christine said, drifting out the door again. "I'm just a secretary."

"Right," Nick said. "And don't you forget it."

Christine ignored him.

"NICK!" PARK HAD COME OUT from behind his massive desk to slap him on the back, the picture of an Ivy League beach-boy, hitting forty and fighting it every minute. "Buddy! Pal! *Compadre!*"

"*Compadre?*" Nick shook his head and stretched out in the leather chair in front of Park's desk. "This must be bad. You don't speak Spanish."

"How about *partner?*" Park said.

Nick crossed his ankles on the Oriental rug, trying to look unconcerned as his pulse leapt. "Partner would be good," he said. "Does this mean we got the Welch account?"

"We haven't *exactly* got the account." Park sat on the edge of his desk and leaned forward to slap Nick on the shoulder again. "But no problemo, hey? You can still pull it off. You'll just have to do a couple of small things and—"

"What?" Nick said suspiciously, his heart sinking at Park's tone.

"Well, it would help if you'd get married," Park said.

"I told you that you shouldn't have done all those drugs in the seventies," Nick said. "You're having a flashback."

"Funny." Park paused. "Welch called Dad. He wants to meet our families. Especially yours. He likes you."

"We don't have families," Nick said. "Or I don't. You can at least show him a couple of parents. What's this about?"

"I have no idea," Park said. "We're invited to his place in Kentucky—Friday night and Saturday—for a reading from his new book, and Dad said that Welch specifically told him that we're supposed to bring our wives. Especially you. What did you say to Welch, anyway?"

Nick shrugged. "I don't know. I sure as hell didn't tell him I was married. He came to my office on an impulse, he said, and for some reason he was being a real bastard, edgy as hell, and I was pouring on the charm, trying to sell him on the deal when all of sudden, he—" Nick stopped, trying to pinpoint exactly what had happened. "He mellowed on me. Smiled, nodded, turned into Mr. Congeniality." Nick frowned as he remembered the conversation. "I've been going over it in my mind, but for the life of me, I can't recall exactly what I said. I was just explaining the plans we had for negotiating the new book contract, and suddenly he was a nice guy. And now he wants to meet my family? This is ridiculous."

"No, this is Norbert Nolan Welch, the great American author," Park said. "This is the account my father wants, has always wanted, and will be overwhelmed to get. This is the one we want so much that if we have to get married to get it, we will."

Nick narrowed his eyes. "Why will we do this?"

Park shifted on the desk. "Because if we get this, my father will retire." He paused for a moment, a look of ecstasy on his face.

"Why?" Nick said.

"He's been trying to get Welch for years." Park shrugged at the inexplicability of it. "He'd consider it going out in style. Leaving the firm after snagging the account of one of America's greatest novelists is his idea of the perfect exit. Think of the speeches at his retirement dinner. Think of the bragging he could do." Park looked guiltily at Nick. "Think of you finally making partner."

Nick straightened in his chair, trying hard not to leap to his feet at the thought. There was ambition, which was good; and then there was pathetic, deep-seated, naked ambition, which was bad and which he was riddled with. He knew it was bad because it made him look anxious and vulnerable, and because Tess had told him it was morally reprehensible and there were times he thought she might have a point. A small point, but still a point. In the long run, though, it didn't matter; lust for success was what made him run, and as long as he didn't actually start maiming people to get to the top, he could live with it. The trick was in not betraying the depth of his need, so he kept his voice as cool as possible as he asked, "I make partner if we sign Welch?"

"No doubt about it," Park said. "We could stop sneaking around trying to run this place behind Dad's back. We could stop cleaning up after his mistakes. And we could definitely make you partner. With my dad retired, it won't matter that you're not family. It won't be a family firm anymore, anyway."

It was exactly what Nick wanted, but like everything else he'd wanted in his life, there was a catch to it. There was always a catch. Sometimes Nick got damn tired of catches.

He leaned back in his chair and shook his head at Park. "But I make partner only if we get the account, which is probably not going to happen, and we both know it. You know, you could just suggest to your father that I should be a partner even though I'm not family. I'm overdue for it, no matter what he says."

Park looked appalled. "Disagree with my father?"

"Right," Nick said. "I forgot. So what is it I have to do here?"

"Get married."

"No."

"My dad thinks it's time." Park looked suicidal. "He said that playing the field is for young men. He said unmarried men at forty-two just look pathetic."

Nick shrugged. "That's your problem. I'm thirty-eight."

"He said anything over thirty-five is questionable."

Nick held on to his patience. "Park, no offense, but I don't give a rat's ass what your father thinks about my marital status. I just want to make partner." He thought for a minute. "And a lot of money."

"And you will," Park assured him. "You just have to get the Welch account."

"Right."

"So find a wife," Park said.

"No."

"How about a serious fiancée? Can't you propose to one of those women you keep dating?"

"How about a serious breach-of-promise suit when I change my mind after the weekend is over?"

"Don't you know anybody who could fake it for a weekend?" Park's eyes pleaded with him. "Dad said we had to get women who know literature."

"Tess," Nick said promptly, and Park groaned.

"Not Tess. Anyone but Tess."

"She probably wouldn't do it, anyway," Nick said. "She pretty much stopped talking to me right after I refused to—" He caught himself and stopped. "What have you got against Tess, anyway?"

"I just hate to see you limiting yourself to one woman. Never limit yourself. That's why I want you to get the Welch account. New horizons."

"I haven't exactly seen everything I wanted of Tess's horizons," Nick said.

"Tess is no good for you," Park said. "Women with brains are bad news. They distract you with their bodies and then they—"

"Tess would be excellent for impressing an author," Nick said. "She's an English teacher. She's involved in all those censorship protests." He thought back to the last one he'd seen her at, holding a sign that said Pornography Is in the Mind of the Beholder. She'd been wearing a blue sweater, and his mind had leapt instantly to pornographic thoughts, which were the safest thoughts he could have around Tess. She was tactless and undignified and spontaneous and out of control, but there was something about her that kept pulling him back to her, and he hoped to hell it was her body, because if it was anything more, he was in big trouble.

Of course, it wasn't anything more. He had a career to protect.

Park was still on the trail. "Protesting might not be good. Is it legal?"

Nick slumped back in his chair. "Park, did you pay any attention in law school?"

"Only to the good stuff. I knew I wasn't going to be defending protesters." Park frowned at him. "What do you see in this woman?"

Nick started to tell him and then stopped. Park would never understand the attraction of Tess's cheerfully passionate need to save the world, although he would probably understand the attraction of her cheerfully passionate enthusiasm for life, an enthusiasm that swept away everyone she was with until they almost did incredibly stupid things in Music Hall parking lots. Things that would have gotten them arrested for public indecency.

He shook his head to get rid of the thought before he lost his mind completely.

Back to Park's question. Stick to the basics. "She has great legs."

Park put his hand on Nick's shoulder and gave him a fatherly pat. "That's not enough to build a relationship on."

"Oh?" Nick said, surprised at this sudden evidence of depth in his friend. "And what is?"

"Breasts," Park said, and Nick had the feeling he was only partly joking. "Breasts are very important for women. Their clothes just don't hang right without them."

Nick nodded. "Thanks, Dad, I'll keep that in mind."

"Although she does have excellent legs," Park went on. "Still, you're better off without—"

"What were you doing looking at Tess's legs? I thought you didn't like her."

"Trust me, as soon as she opened her mouth, I stopped looking. What did you do—gag her at night?"

Nick briefly considered explaining that he'd never spent the night, and then discarded the idea. It would open a whole new conversational distraction for Park, and after his father's pep talk, Park was distracted enough already.

Park went back on attack. "You can pull this off for one weekend. Just don't get Tess to do it. That mouth of hers makes me nervous. She has absolutely no tact, and she always tells the truth no matter who she's talking to." He shook his head in disgusted amazement. "Definitely not our kind of people."

Nick looked at his friend with resignation. "Why do I get the feeling that if I stick with you, one day I'll wake up with my hair slicked back, wearing red suspenders and muttering, 'Greed is good'?"

"There's nothing wrong with greed," Park said. "In moderation, of course. Now, go get a date for this weekend. And remember Welch is an author. She has to have read something besides the society pages."

"Really? Then who the hell are you going to bring?" Nick asked.

"Oh. Good point," Park said, and frowned. "Can you get me a date?"

2

"LET ME GET this straight," Tess said from her armchair when Nick had finished explaining and the only evidence left of the pot stickers was an empty carton and a tangy memory. "You want me to pretend to be your fiancée in order to deceive one of our greatest living American authors so that you can take another step in your drive toward ultimate yuppiehood." She thought about it for a minute. "This could be good. I could wear an apron."

Nick looked confused. "No, you couldn't. This is a very ritzy party. Why would you wear an apron?"

Tess shrugged. "All right, no apron. But it's your loss."

Nick shifted slightly. "Tess, concentrate here. I need to look like somebody who is approaching commitment. You need to act like somebody I'd commit to. Can you pull this off?" He squinted at her. "Of course you can't. Why don't I ever listen to Park?"

"Because he's an idiot," Tess said. "Did he tell you I couldn't do this? The rat. I know you bonded in college, but haven't you noticed what a valueless twit he is?"

"Valueless is a little harsh," Nick said. "Immature, maybe."

"What did he do? Pull you from a burning building?" Tess shook her head. "Lassie wasn't this faithful to Timmy."

"He does all right by me," Nick said. "And he pulls his own weight with the firm. Park may have his limits, but believe it or not, he's a genius with contracts. And yes, I owe him. The only reason I'm even with the firm is that Park hauled me in with him."

"I understand that," Tess said patiently. "And I admire your loyalty. But since then you've pulled him out of a jam how many times? Don't you think you're about paid up here? Especially since he's trashing your fiancée." When Nick seemed puzzled, she added patiently, "That would be me, remember?"

"Right," Nick said. "At least, I remember when I thought that was a good idea. Look, I haven't pulled Park out of a jam that many times. And we're doing all right together. Hell, we could be rich if we nail this Welch account."

"You're already rich," Tess said. "It's time to move to a higher plane. Get a new interest. One with values."

"I have values." Nick cast a disgusted look around the apartment. "Besides, if this is the kind of life you get for having values, I'll pass. This place is a dump. And where the hell did you get those sweats, anyway? They're older than you are."

"Hey," Tess said, annoyed at having to defend her sweats yet one more time. "I paid for these with honest money at an honest thrift store." She stuck her chin in the air. "Just because, unlike you and *Park*, I don't buy overpriced designer *running togs* that I never *run* in because I might get *sweaty*—"

"Wait a minute," Nick said. "I run."

But Tess was already warming to the drama of the moment. "—which would be a waste of the *ill-gotten gains* I used to buy them—"

"I object to the ill-gotten gains—"

"Always a lawyer," Tess said. "Objection overruled."

"Look, we don't cheat widows and orphans or defend rapists or polluters or do any of those other things you tree huggers are always on about," Nick fumed. "We're lawyers, not criminals, for cripe's sake. Cut me a break."

Tess came down from her high horse. "Sorry," she said. "I got a little carried away." She looked at him, biting her lip. "This is like déjà vu. This is every argument we ever had."

"I know," Nick said gloomily. "It was the only good thing about not seeing you anymore. I didn't have to have this stupid argument."

"Well, you don't have to have it now," Tess said. "The door is over there. And this engagement would never have worked for us, anyway. You wouldn't have let me wear an apron, and as the years went by, I would have resented it. Then one day, I'd have picked up a meat cleaver and there we'd be, in the *National Enquirer*, just like John and Lorena." Nick blinked at her, and she took pity on him and dropped her story. "Well, thanks for stopping by. See you." She waited for him to get up and leave, feeling absolutely miserable for the first time since the last time she'd left him.

Nick put his head against the wall and closed his eyes. "I can't leave. I need you." He opened his eyes and met hers squarely. "This could get me a partnership, Tess."

Tess felt a stab of sympathy for him. "Oh, love. When are you going to stop trying to prove you're the best? You don't have to sweat like this anymore. Your picture is on the society page all the time. You're a Riverbend celebrity. People adore you. You've made it."

Nick shook his head. "Not till I've made partner. I know that in your eyes that makes me an immoral, profiteering, capitalist whoremonger, but I will not be happy until I've made partner. I've worked a long time for this, and I *want* it."

"I know." Tess frowned. "What I don't know is why Park isn't giving it to you."

Nick let his head fall back against the wall again. "Because Park can't. His father still runs the firm, and Park would walk naked in traffic before he'd confront him or, God forbid, disagree with him. But Park swears his father will retire if we get the Welch account, and then Park can make me partner."

Tess was confused. "Why doesn't his father want to make you partner? You're brilliant. And you practically run that firm now. This doesn't make sense. You *deserve* partner."

"His father cares about background," Nick said stiffly. "Mine is blue-collar. Not the kind of person to be a partner in a Patterson law firm."

Tess looked dumbfounded. "You're kidding. He can't be that archaic."

"Sure he can," Nick said. "It's his law firm. He can be anything he wants."

Tess slumped back in her chair and considered Nick and what she owed him. The first time they'd met, he'd knocked her on her butt playing touch football, and then sat on her to make her give up the ball, doing terrible Bogart impressions until she'd surrendered because she was weak from laughing. When she broke up with the guy she'd been dating a month later, she'd called Nick trying not to cry, and he'd brought her chocolate ice cream and *Terms of Endearment* on video, and then kept her company while she sobbed through the movie. And he'd never said anything about the mascara she'd left all over his shirt. And today he'd known she was upset about something and brought her pot stickers.

On the other hand, he worshiped money and success, and he'd humiliated her by rejecting her in a parking lot.

They were almost even. But not quite. Because no matter how sure she was that she was finished with him as a romantic possibility—and she was pretty sure, she told herself—he was a friend. If friends needed you, you came through. That was the rule.

Tess felt the prison doors begin to close on her. "Oh, damn," she muttered.

Nick leaned forward and gave her his best smile, the one that made him look boyish and vulnerable. "I have no right to ask you this, but will you do it? For me? Even though you don't owe me anything?"

Tess bit her lip. He looked so sweet sitting there. And sexy. Of course, she knew that he knew he looked boyish and vulnerable and sweet and sexy because that was the effect he was going for, but deep, deep, *deep* down inside, he really was a sweet man. He just had a lousy peer group.

And if she did it, she'd get to be with him again.

"Okay, I'll do it," Tess said.

Nick slumped in relief. "Thank God." He grinned up at her. "I don't suppose you could get Park a date, too? Somebody respectable?"

"You're kidding."

"Somebody at the Foundation?" Nick said. "Somebody who reads?"

"I'll ask around," Tess said. "I will have to mention that he's worthless, of course."

"Great." Nick stood up to go. "Listen, if there's anything I can do for you, just name it. I owe you big for this."

"Good. Introduce me to somebody on the board of the Decker Academy."

Nick gaped at her. "Why?"

"I lost my job," Tess said, and Nick sat down again.

"I knew something was wrong. I'm sorry, Tess. What happened?"

"Funding cuts," Tess said. His sympathy was so unexpectedly comforting that she lost her emotional balance for a moment, but then she took a deep breath and grinned at him. "But it's all right. I met this really nice man at the last censorship protest."

Nick scowled at her. "Do not talk to strange men, dummy."

"And we talked for a long time, and he was darling," Tess said, ignoring his scowl. "And he said if I ever needed a job, to call him, because I was obviously a great teacher."

"And this has what to do with the Decker Academy?" Nick said, still scowling.

"He's in charge of it," Tess said. "His name is Alan—"

"Sigler," Nick finished. "He must be sixty. What are you doing flirting with older men?"

"But I told him I don't have a teaching certificate. And he said that was bad because the board would have to vote to make an exception in my case, and they weren't very open to change, so I thought if you knew any of them . . ."

"I do," Nick said thoughtfully. "In fact, a couple of them may be at this Welch thing this weekend. He's big on upper-class education for some reason." He frowned at her. "Dress conservatively. These people are not cutting edge." He thought for another moment, and Tess watched him contemplate her problem, turning it over in his mind, examining it from every angle as if it was something important to his career, instead of hers, and she felt comforted again. "I'll do what I can," he said finally. "I just don't understand why you want to work at Decker. All those rich kids?"

"The pay is good," Tess said. "And the school day ends at one o'clock so they can work on special projects or something."

Nick snorted. "Country Club 101."

"I don't care. I could be back at the Foundation by one-thirty. A lot of my kids don't come in for help until then."

Nick frowned at her. "Two jobs? What are you trying to do—kill yourself?"

Tess stuck her chin out. "I can't leave the Foundation. They need me. The kids need me. I know you don't understand, but they need me."

Nick was silent for a moment. "All right," he said finally. "Let me see what I can do." He stood up and then looked down at her, the worry clear in his eyes. "But you have to promise me that you won't work yourself into the ground if you get this job."

Tess bit her lip. "See, this is what makes me crazy about you," she said. "Say something materialistic so I can get my guard up again."

"Your sweats are awful," Nick said. "But your face looks like a million dollars." He bent to kiss her, and Tess felt the little shock of lust he always sparked in her as his mouth covered hers and his tongue tickled her lips. He tasted of pot stickers and beer and Nick, and she smiled against his cheek when he moved his head to bite her earlobe.

"Charmer," she whispered against his ear, and he grinned and kissed her again, and she felt the warmth from his lips seep into her bones.

When he was gone, she stared into space for a while, wondering what she was getting herself into. Nick was a darling, she reminded herself, but he was also dedicated to one person and one person only—Nick. He liked her a lot, but he'd cheerfully dump her in a minute if it meant making partner in that damn firm.

So don't go fantasizing about him, she told herself sternly. She'd just use him to meet the Decker people and get him to pull any strings he had to get her the job. She wasn't going to start thinking about his arms again. That always led to scattered thinking, and she still had to decide what to do about Gina, how to protect the other tenants, how to save the Foundation, how to get the job at Decker...

Tess curled up in the chair and put her head on her knees and thought about how good it would feel to be in Nick's arms again. When her thoughts drifted from security in his arms to making love in his arms, she groaned and reached for the phone and dialed Gina's number.

No sense in suffering alone.

"You're gonna do it?" Gina asked when Tess told her about Nick's proposal.

"Of course I'm going to do it." Tess cradled the phone to her ear as she slumped back in her chair. "He needs me. He can be a materialistic jerk and a womanizer, but deep inside he's a nice guy and he needs me." She shifted in the chair, searching for a better justification for seeing him again. "He probably doesn't really want to do this. It's that louse Park."

Gina sounded doubtful. "I don't think it's all this Park's fault. Nick's a big boy. He could say no."

"Nick can't say no to Park. He's been baby-sitting Park since college and it's gotten to be a habit." Tess's frown turned into a grin as she thought about it. "You wouldn't believe how they met." She sat up in her chair as she warmed to her story. "Nick told me he was tutoring in college as part of a work-study program, and Park showed up, on the verge of getting kicked out of school because of this really important English lit paper he'd flunked. On *Moby Dick*."

"That's the whale, right? I saw the movie."

"Right," Tess said. "Only when Park showed Nick the paper, the prof had written across the top of it, 'Unfortunately, Mr. Patterson, the whale dies in the end.'"

"Park didn't know the whale died?" Gina sounded confused. "He died in the movie."

"Yeah, he dies in the Cliff Notes, too," Tess said, laughing. "So Nick said he asked Park how he could possibly have missed that part, and Park said that when he was a kid, his parents only bought him educational toys, and one of the games they bought him was the Moby Dick game—"

"The Moby Dick *game?*"

"—but the game was meant for kids, so in the game—"

"The whale makes it," Gina finished.

"Exactly," Tess said, dissolving into laughter. "And Park wrote the paper based on what he knew from the game. Isn't that hysterical?"

"No," Gina said. "I think it's sad. Why did his parents only buy him educational stuff?"

"Because his parents want him to be God," Tess said, slumping down in the chair. "And Park doesn't have the brains to make cherub. So he leans on Nick, and Nick carries the whole firm. And that's why I hate Park Patterson. If it hadn't been for Park, Nick would probably have ended up as a district attorney, doing something decent for humanity, instead of running around pampering rich people. He's so brilliant. It's such a waste."

"It's his choice," Gina said. "And so is this Welch thing. I don't think you can blame Park."

"I can blame Park," Tess said. "He's the one who made this such a big deal. He promised Nick he'll make partner if they get this account."

Gina sounded unconvinced. "So why do you care? I thought you spit on big business. Especially lawyer big business."

"I do. Nick doesn't. And he needs my help."

"So you're still hung up on him."

"No, I'm not hung up on him." Tess sat up again, annoyed. "I just feel sorry for him."

"Right," Gina said. "And?"

"And he makes me feel good." Tess leaned back a little as she thought about it. "Okay, he makes me feel really good."

"And?" Gina prodded.

"And he turns me on," Tess finally admitted, sliding all the way back down into the chair. "I know, I'm shallow." She sighed. "Really shallow. I know he's a mercenary lawyer, but we're talking about a man who turns me on doing his laundry. You know, the kind of guy you sit next to by the dryer, and he's wearing a sweatshirt with the sleeves cut off, and you realize he has the best arms you've ever seen in your life, and suddenly you're having hot flashes and losing your train of thought, and it's either menopause complicated by Alzheimer's or you're in heat, and then that damn tingle starts and you know you're in heat, and you have to go upstairs and lock the door, because if you don't, you'll claw off his shirt and bite into his bicep."

After a long pause Gina said, "Would you like me to wait while you go take a cold shower?"

Tess ignored the question. "This is why I should not be seeing him again. Because it's only a matter of time before I just drag him off to the nearest flat surface and have my way with him. And that would be bad."

"Oh, yeah," Gina said. "That sounds bad. I wish I had something that bad."

"Look," Tess said, "don't get snippy on me. That *would* be bad. I mean, I'm already tempted by him just because he makes me laugh and feel safe. If I went to bed with him and it was great, I'd be in real trouble. Because as much as he makes me crazy with lust, he really isn't right for me. He thinks my apartment is a dump, and he gets huffy about my thrift-store clothes, and he wears designer suits and gold watches."

"Oh, well, gold watches," Gina said. "There's a real drawback."

"It's symbolic," Tess protested. "I mean, he can be really sweet, but he can also be an uptight, money-hungry yuppie. And the thing is, those money-hungry times just seem to be getting longer and the sweet times shorter, and I don't really believe you can change a guy, and who am I to decide to change him, anyway? He's happy the way he is. We're better off apart. Besides, he won't let me wear an apron."

Gina sighed. "I think you should lose your mind and marry him. God knows, I would. I'm the one who needs somebody to support me."

"How very mercenary of you," Tess said.

"How very practical of me," Gina said. "So how old is this Park?"

"Oh, come on."

"Come on, yourself. How old?"

"Late thirties, early forties, I think," Tess said. "Nick's thirty-eight, and I think Park's a few years older."

"I like older guys."

"Gina!" Tess sat up and clutched the phone. "After all I've said about him? You wouldn't."

"Of course I wouldn't," Gina said, laughing. "I'm just yanking your chain. Can't you just see me with some high-society guy? What a laugh."

"Why?" Tess said, switching sides in an instant. "What's wrong with you in high society? You'd fit in anywhere. In fact, now that I think about it, you'd be great for Park." She started to grin as she thought about it. "He always dates these women who have the personalities of flatfish. It would do him good to meet a real female person."

"Forget it."

"I'm not kidding." Tess examined her new idea and liked it. "Listen, if you're not busy this weekend, I can get you invited to a party full of rich guys with husband potential, and you'll get to see Park in action because you'll be his date."

"God, no," Gina said, the horror in her voice evident even over the phone. "Rich guys? I don't want a rich guy. I'd stick out like a sore thumb."

"What are you talking about?" Tess said. "You would not. And speaking of sticking out, what was the deal with the gum? You only chew gum when you get nervous. What happened?"

"Nick kinda makes me nervous," Gina said. "It's not his fault. He just always looks so . . . slick. You know?"

"I know," Tess said gloomily as she sank back into her chair.

"Listen, I appreciate this, I really do," Gina said, her words tumbling out in a nervous rush, "but I can't go to this thing with you. I'd die, I really would."

"No, you won't. I'll be with you. Besides, you need this. You want a husband, you're going to get one. This place will be crawling with rich guys. One of them might be nice. If nothing else, you'll get a whole weekend of free food."

"I don't need food that much."

"Besides, it's just Park," Tess said. "He has the brains of a kumquat. You'll do fine."

"I don't know," Gina said.

"I'll give his secretary your number," Tess said. "This is going to be great for you."

"Gee, thanks," Gina said. "I don't know about this, Tess."

"Trust me," Tess said. "This is going to be the best thing that ever happened to you."

3

FOR THE NEXT TWO DAYS Tess tutored at the Foundation, researched the backgrounds and interests of everyone on the board of the Decker Academy and tried to forget Nick and the upcoming weekend. Forgetting Nick was not easy. She reminded herself that he had patted Gina on the head and made her nervous enough to chew gum. But then she reminded herself that he'd rushed Angela to the vet when she'd been hit by a car even though she'd scratched him and bled all over his leather jacket and he'd never said a word to her in reproach. And then she remembered that he had the greatest arms she'd ever seen on a man. And then her mind wandered and she was in trouble again. In fact, her mind wandered a lot, and it always wandered to Nick, and her thoughts were always eventually more than warm no matter how she tried to talk herself out of them, and they often led to her lying curled in the fetal position on her couch contemplating hotly inappropriate acts in excitingly inappropriate places with a consenting conservative lawyer.

By Thursday, she was regretting she'd ever met him and counting the hours until she saw him again.

NICK WOULD HAVE understood perfectly.

"This may have been a mistake," he told Christine Thursday morning when she brought the mail into his office and dropped it on his massive ebony desk.

"Probably," Christine agreed. "Park left a message. He has a date for tomorrow night with someone who can read. He said to tell you thank-you."

"What do you mean 'probably'?" Nick demanded, tipping his leather desk chair back so he could meet her eyes. "You don't even know what I'm talking about."

"You're not sure about Tess," Christine said.

"How'd you know that?" Nick narrowed his eyes suspiciously. "You know, sometimes you're a little creepy, Christine."

"I live to serve," she said.

Nick stared at her for a moment, biting his lip, tapping his pen on the desktop. "It's not just her mouth," he said finally. "It's her clothes. She's completely capable of wrapping herself in a thrift-store tablecloth and calling it a Victorian sarong."

Christine waited, staring into space as if mentally doing her nails.

"Christine..." Nick began, smiling at her with all the charm in his possession.

Christine buffed another mental cuticle.

"Yo, Christine," Nick said, snapping his fingers.

"I'm here," Christine said. "Waiting for orders. Any orders."

"You know, Christine," Nick said, "the life of a secretary is a . . . *varied* one."

"What do you want me to do?" Christine said flatly.

Nick gave up on the charm. "I know this isn't in your job description, but go get Tess a dress and have it delivered to her. Then take the rest of the afternoon off so I don't feel guilty about making you shop instead of type. I'm not going to get a damn thing done until this party is over, anyway."

Christine stood patiently. "Where, what size, what color?"

Nick took a card out of his desk and began to write. "I don't care where. I don't know what size. Black. Conservative." He finished writing and handed her the card. "Put that with it."

Christine read the card. "I need to know the size."

Nick frowned. "Sort of medium."

Christine looked at him with contempt, which Nick saw as a move in the right direction, given Christine's general detachment from human interaction.

"How tall is she?" Christine asked.

"Oh...about here," Nick said, slicing his hand at ear level.

"About five eight," Christine guessed. "How much does she weigh?"

"I don't know," Nick said. "She's not fat, but she's upholstered. You know, soft not bony." He looked confused. "She's medium."

"Breasts?" Christine asked.

"Yes."

"No, how big are they?"

Nick frowned up at her, trying not to think about Tess's breasts. He had two whole days to get through, and he was distracted enough already. "They're, uh, sort of more than medium, I guess. Do we have to talk about this?"

"She's a ten, a twelve or a fourteen."

"Split the difference—go for the twelve."

"Fine," Christine said, and drifted toward the door, the card in her hand.

"Hey," Nick said. "Would you like some money to pay for this?"

"No," Christine said at the door. "I'll put it on your Visa."

Nick blinked. "Can you do that?"

Christine smiled at him serenely and left.

"Hey, Christine," Nick called after her. "If you ever turn to a life of crime, remember I was good to you. Christine?"

Nothing but silence answered him, so he returned to the problem at hand. How much of a liability was Tess going to be at this party? The more he thought about it, the more depressed he got. Asking Tess had been dumb, and sticking her in an expensive black dress was not going to help things much. Not unless he got her an expensive black gag to go with it. *This is what happens when you let your emotions take over*, he railed at himself. Just because he wanted to see her again—only all of her this time—he'd asked her to a career-making weekend. *The career comes first*, he reminded himself. *Don't forget that again.*

Then he went back to worrying.

LATER THAT AFTERNOON, the glitziest department store in town delivered a package to Tess.

The underfed messenger pumped his Adam's apple and looked around nervously as he stood in the hall outside her apartment. "Jeez, lady," he said. "You really live here?"

"Don't be a wimp," Tess told him, but she tipped him more than she could afford anyway, resisting the impulse to offer him food instead. Then she took the box into the apartment and opened it.

Nick had sent her a black crepe dress. It came below her knee and laced at the sides with black crepe laces that blended so well with the fabric that they were practically invisible. The dress was beautifully if conservatively cut, and Tess hated it on sight. When she tried it on, she hated it even more. It fit perfectly when the laces were tightened, and it made her look respectable and successful. She wanted to kill Nick, but she called Gina to come over instead.

"Stop bitching," Gina told her when she got to Tess's apartment. "He probably knew you didn't have anything for this kind of shindig. He was being thoughtful."

"Wait'll you see this thing," Tess said, dragging her into the bedroom.

But all Gina said when she saw the dress was, "It's beautiful. It really was thoughtful, Tess."

"Thoughtful, my hat. He's being patronizing. He thinks I don't have anything decent."

Gina looked around Tess's bedroom, which was furnished with a creaky bed, a dozen thrift-store pillows and Angela, and raised an eyebrow at her.

Tess grinned and flapped a hand. "That's not what I meant. I meant he's assuming I didn't have anything decent to *wear*."

"You don't." Gina dropped onto the bed and looked at the dress wistfully before she returned to her attack. "Look, Tess, he did his laundry with you. He knows what your clothes look like. He knows what you dress like. He did you a favor. What'd the card say?"

"What card?"

"There must have been a card." Gina sounded exasperated as she reached for the box and pawed through the tissue paper until she found it. "Got it. It says . . ." She hesitated while she pulled it out. "It says, 'I saw this and knew you'd look great in it. Thank you for saving my life. Nick.'" Gina frowned at Tess. "And you're not planning on hanging on to him? You're nuts. I'd kill to have somebody write me cards like this."

"That's because you don't know him like I do," Tess grumbled. "I mean, look at this dress. Nancy Reagan would love this dress. He's trying to make me a Republican for the weekend."

"Nancy Reagan dressed great," Gina said. "You're such a bigot. If it's Republican, you want to burn a cross in the yard. Shape up." She looked at the dress wistfully again. "It would be nice to have clothes like that, you know? Real clothes, not just cheap stuff."

Tess looked at the dress dubiously. "I suppose so." She pulled at it a little, growing more cheerful as she studied it. "It's just one night. And then maybe I can change the laces and lower the neckline."

"And put a slit up the side and pretend you're Suzie Wong," Gina added. "Why don't you just give respectability a try?"

"Never," Tess said. "You'll know I'm dead when I start acting respectable."

"Somehow I'm not worried," Gina said. "Listen, all I've got for this thing is my black jersey dress. You know, the one with the belt? Is that gonna be okay?"

"Sure." Tess shrugged. "You look great in everything."

"It's not like this," Gina said, fingering the material of Tess's dress one more time before she let go. "It's not the kinda dress that people just look at and know it's a good dress."

"Gina, you look so darling in everything you put on that people don't care what you're wearing," Tess said as she turned to hang the dress on the back of the closet door. "Forget about your dress. You'll look great." She turned back to Gina. "I'll wrap that thing in plastic tonight and pack my duffel so we can leave right after school. Nick's picking me up at four. You're riding with Park, right?"

"You're not going to be late, are you?" Gina said, sudden panic making her voice sharp. "Please."

"You're not even riding down with us," Tess said. "What difference does it make to you whether I'm late or not?"

"All those people." Gina clutched her hands together. "I want them to think I'm classy. I need you near me."

"Not if you want people to think you're classy," Tess said, and shut the closet door on the Nancy Reagan dress.

NICK WAS NOT at all surprised that Tess wasn't home when he came to pick her up on Friday afternoon. He put his suitcase by the door and rang the bell, and when there was no answer, he leaned against the wall to wait. Tess was always late because she always got caught up in the drama of the moment wherever she was. Time was relative to Einstein and Tess alike.

While he waited, he thought about Tess and all the ways she could screw up his life, particularly this weekend. The more he thought about Tess and her cheerful bluntness, the more tense he got. He closed his eyes and thought about calling the whole thing off, and then he thought about Tess and spending the weekend with Tess and—if he laid his plans carefully—spending the night with Tess. *The career comes first*, he reminded himself, but then he also reminded himself that man did not live by career alone. At least she'd be dressed well for the party, and as long as he never left her side maybe he could stop her from actually ruining his life, and besides, he wanted to be with her. He missed her. Okay, the weekend with Welch was probably not the best place to renew Tess's acquaintance, but it was all he had. There was no point in obsessing over her unpredictability. That was the penalty for being with Tess. Tess would stop being spontaneous when she stopped being sloppy and late, and that would be never. Sometimes he thought that was one of the reasons he missed having her around—her chaos had been a sort of relief from his carefully mapped-out life. Not that there was anything wrong with a carefully mapped-out life. He'd spent twenty years carefully weighing his every option and it had gotten him everything he'd ever wanted.

Except partner.

Well, he'd have that soon, too. If it took getting the Welch account, he'd get it, even if he had to bind and gag Tess to do it. And then he'd have everything he'd ever wanted.

And then what?

Nick considered his future.

He'd been thinking about Park's father's theory that unmarried men over thirty-five were pathetic. Park's father was wrong, of course, but he might have a point if he changed the age limit to forty. That was two years away for Nick. It might actually be time to start thinking marriage. It wasn't as if he hadn't wanted to get married. He had. Eventually. When his career was in place. When he found the right woman.

But now he might make partner. And if he did, he'd need somebody to be a hostess, somebody to open the door of his house and welcome people in, somebody to call the caterers. It occurred to him that if Christine could develop some expression, it would probably be easiest just to upgrade her status to wife. God knew, she was undemanding and efficient. Unfortunately she was also Morticia Addams without the enthusiasm.

What he needed was a cross between Christine and Tess.

He thought about being married to Tess and grinned. Of course, she'd have to get different clothes, and he'd have to get his housekeeper to come every day to pick up after her, and she'd have to learn to shut up when it was politically necessary, but she'd also be around all the time, laughing, warming his life, warming his bed . . .

It was a thought with definite promise.

He heard the door slam downstairs, and then someone pounding up the three flights to Tess's floor, and then Tess herself surged into view, stopping in her tracks when she saw him.

She looked like a Gap ad, although he knew better than to tell her that. Her short red hair curled around her pale face, and her eyes were huge and placating as she smiled at him in apology. Her oversize navy T-shirt hung just to her hips over a navy cotton mini skirt, and she was wearing that god-awful baggy navy tweed jacket she loved. It was worn so thin that it fluttered as she walked toward him, but for once, he didn't care. He felt good just looking at her.

Suddenly the thought of a life with her had a lot more promise.

"I'm sorry," she said when she reached him. "I really am."

"Relax," he said, keeping his arms folded so he wouldn't reach for her. "We've got time."

Tess stopped and put her hands on her hips. "You said four at the latest."

"That's because I knew you'd be late." Nick looked at his Rolex. "But now we do have to get moving. Tell me you're packed."

"I'm packed," Tess said, giving up as she moved past him to unlock her door. "I can't believe you set me up like this."

Nick picked up his suitcase and followed her into the apartment. "So what was it? No, let me guess. You were at the Foundation. Some kid needed help."

Tess grinned at him. "All right. Big deal. You know me."

"Remember that." Nick looked around and sighed when he saw her bulging duffel on the couch. "I thought so. Give me that damn thing. I am not taking that to Kentucky." Tess handed him the bag, and he frowned at her jacket. Her clothes were impossible. "Could we lose the jacket, too, just for the weekend?"

"Oh, don't be so snotty." Tess smoothed her worn sleeve with love. "This is a great jacket. It's very practical and it never wears out. And it has memories."

"Probably more than you do," Nick said. "It's been around a lot longer than you have." He dumped the duffel on Tess's rickety dining-room table and opened his suitcase beside it. Then he began transferring her clothes to his suitcase. "Of course, on you the jacket looks great, but anything looks great on you."

"Save the snake oil." Tess grinned at him. "I love this jacket. It's me. I'm wearing it."

"Okay, fine. Whatever makes you happy." Nick folded the last of her clothes into the suitcase and closed it. "Now, we're ready."

"If you say so." Tess shook her head. "But the duffel would have been a lot easier."

"Not on my eyes." Nick picked up the suitcase. "Not to mention my dignity."

Tess's smile widened. "You have no dignity."

"Not around you." Nick grinned back at her, suddenly warmed by how alive she was just standing in front of him and suddenly damn glad to be with her. "This is why we should be together. You can save me from getting too stuffy."

"Fine for you," Tess folded her arms and looked at him with mock skepticism. "Who's going to save me?"

"I am," Nick said. "Hell, woman, can't you recognize a hero when you've got one in your living room?"

"This would be you?" Tess lifted an eyebrow.

"This would be me. Picture me in armor. Better yet picture me out of armor making love to you."

Tess stopped and blinked at him, and Nick's smile grew evil.

"No," Tess said. "Don't be ridiculous."

Nick shook his head. "Good thing for you I'm a patient man."

"That's not necessarily good for me."

Nick laughed. "Okay, be that way. Could we get going here? I'd like to have at least a couple of hubcaps left for the ride home. Why are you still living in this dump, anyway? The crime rate around here must be out of control."

"It is not." Tess suddenly looked guilty enough to make Nick wonder if the crime rate really was bad enough to worry her. "And besides," she plunged on, "if you didn't bring an overpriced car into a deprived neighborhood, you wouldn't have to worry about some kid heisting your hubcaps to even out the economic imbalance. So there."

Nick felt his familiar Tess-annoyance rise again. "So you're saying that some delinquent is justified in stealing my hubcaps because he doesn't have as much money as I do?" Nick shifted the suitcase to his right hand to keep from strangling her. "Situational ethics, right?"

"I'm only saying—" Tess began, and then Nick remembered the weekend and held up his hand.

"Wait a minute," he said. "We have to get through two days together. You look terrific, I look terrific, we like each other a lot when we're not arguing, and we have a strong sexual attraction that I, for one, think we should act on, so why don't we just agree not to mention politics until, oh, say, midnight on Sunday?"

"What sexual attraction? I don't feel any sexual attraction." Tess looked away from him. "And I didn't say you looked terrific."

"Well, I do, don't I?"

TESS LOOKED BACK at him reluctantly, already knowing she was lost. He was beautiful, neatly pressed into a suit that evidently had no seams at all, every strand of his dark hair immaculately in place. Only his face betrayed any sign of human weakness, mainly because he was grinning at her. It was that grin that got her every time. The suit and the haircut belonged to Nick the lawyer, the yuppie materialist. Him, she could resist, no problem. But the grin belonged to Nick the guy who watched old movies with her and handed her tissues when she cried. It belonged to Nick the guy who did the worst Bogart imitation in the world and who knew it and did it anyway. It belonged to Nick the guy who'd gotten one of her students out of trouble with the police when he'd been caught vandalizing the school, and who'd then put the fear of God into the kid so he'd never pick up another can of spray paint again.

The grin kept telling her that the real Nick was trapped inside the designer-suited, I'm-making-partner-before-forty Nick. Maybe that was why she kept fantasizing, against her will, about getting that designer suit off him.

She surrendered and moved toward the door. "All right, you're terrific. I'm sorry I'm being bitchy. I'm nervous about this weekend. I don't want to let you down."

"You won't," Nick said.

Tess shook her head. "I'm not good at lying. Or at being submissive. And I think Norbert Welch is an obnoxious cynic who relieves his insecurities by deliberately annoying everyone with his smug novels. I probably shouldn't mention that this weekend, though."

"Probably not," Nick said. "But you probably will, anyway." He sounded resigned, but not glum. In fact, he seemed pretty buoyant.

"You're really optimistic about this, aren't you?" Tess said, smiling because he seemed so genuinely happy. "You really think this is going to work."

"I'm just glad to be with you again. I missed you."

Tess stopped smiling. "Oh."

"I know." Nick leaned against the wall, the suitcase dangling from one hand. "Don't say it. You've been doing perfectly well without me."

"No, I've missed you, too," Tess admitted. "I hate it, but I have."

"I know you have," Nick said. "I am amazed you admit it, though."

"I'm trying to remember whether it was your confidence or your politics that annoyed me more," Tess said.

"Forget that," Nick said. "Concentrate on what drew you to me."

Tess picked up the hanger that held her plastic-wrapped dress and walked past him to the door. "That would be your companionship, which gave me the ability to do my laundry in the basement without being mugged."

"Resist all you want," Nick said, following her out. "It's not going to do you any good. You're with the best, babe."

He grinned when she snorted in mock disgust and locked the door behind them.

4

THE RIDE TO KENTUCKY in the late September afternoon was lovely, and Tess let her mind wander, lulled by the warm sunlight that was slowly changing to cool dusk outside her window. Nick's car, a black Cobra, was too expensive and too ostentatious, but it rode like a dream, and she snuggled deeper into the seat, loving the comfort of the butter-soft leather.

"I love this car," she said finally.

Nick looked at her in surprise. "Really? This grossly expensive symbol of conspicuous consumption? I don't believe it."

"Well, it is that. But that doesn't mean it isn't sweet." She turned her head to look at him. "I like being with you, too, you know. When you're like this. I could ride this way forever."

"I knew you'd be putty in my hands," Nick said. "Play your cards right, sweetheart, and I'll give you a ride home, too."

"You do the worst Bogart in the world."

"Yeah, but I'm getting better."

"Yeah, but it's still the worst."

Nick grinned over at her, and Tess felt her heart lurch a little. *Stop that*, she told herself.

"You know, I think this idea you have of working at Decker is great," Nick said, as he swung onto the bridge at the Ohio River. "It would be a great career move for you."

"It's not a career move," Tess said, craning her neck like a little kid to look out at the water. "I just need to support myself so I can work at the Foundation."

"You know, I don't understand that," Nick said. "Teaching is teaching. The only difference between the Foundation and Decker is that at Decker you'll get paid a decent salary and—here's a bonus—you won't get mugged."

"No," Tess said. "The difference is that the kids at the Foundation need me more than the kids at Decker. But they're all kids, so it'll be all right. I like kids." She frowned down at the river. "You know, I think I'd like to live on a houseboat."

"And Decker is a big step up," Nick went on. "If Sigler likes you, you could easily move into administration—"

"I'd die first," Tess said. "How do houseboats work exactly? I mean, the plumbing."

"—and with your brains and focus you could be running the place in a year," Nick finished. "I think this is just what you needed to get your life together."

"What?" Tess said. "Running what place?"

"You, in administration at Decker," Nick repeated. "Great idea."

Tess shook her head in disbelief. "Let me out of this car."

"What?" Nick said, startled. "What's wrong now?"

"Listen to me, very carefully," Tess said. "I do not want to run the Decker Academy. I want to teach at the Foundation where I make a difference. To do that, I will do almost anything, but I will not, under any circumstances, become an administrator and stand around in a suit. Suits make me itch. Is that clear?"

Nick shrugged. "Sure. It was just a thought."

"You have terrible thoughts," Tess said. "Keep them to yourself. Now about my houseboat . . ."

"You have a houseboat?" Nick said. "Since when do you have a houseboat? What are you talking about?"

"And they say communication is the foundation of a good marriage," Tess said sadly. "We're doomed. Of course, I knew that. The apron was a big tip-off."

"I don't get the apron thing, either," Nick said. "Is this some Betty Crocker fantasy?"

"I was thinking about baking pie and then making love on the kitchen table."

"You can bake pie?" Nick asked, incredulous.

"No," Tess said. "I told you, it was a fantasy."

"Right," Nick said. "But you *can* make love on a kitchen table. I think that needs more discussion. Like later, in my kitchen."

"I can make love in the front seat of a car, too," Tess said. "Not that you'll ever know, Mr. Conservative."

"Speaking of conservative," Nick said, hastily changing the subject, "thanks for getting Park a date."

"Oh," Tess said innocently. "Did you talk to him? What did he say about her?"

"Nothing." Nick cast a suspicious glance at her. "What did you do? Who is this woman?"

"Oh, don't worry," Tess said. "This is a woman who can handle any situation. She'll be whatever Park needs her to be." She stopped at the idea. "Within reason. Park wouldn't make a pass on a first date, would he?"

Sure, he would, Nick thought, but he said, "Of course not. Stop worrying."

"Tell me about this partnership deal," Tess said before he could ask any more questions, and Nick smiled and began to discuss the implications of getting his name on the door.

TWO HOURS LATER, dusk had settled over Kentucky, and they were at Welch's country place, a gem of a white house ringed by rolling hills and white fences and so many beautiful horses that Tess fully expected to see the young Liz Taylor sobbing into a mane at any minute.

"It looks like a movie set," Tess said as Nick pulled the Cobra into the long lane.

"*The Long Hot Summer*," Nick said. "Great movie."

"With Welch as Will Varner?" Tess considered it. "Could work."

"Sure," Nick said. "And I'll do the Paul Newman part and you can do Joanne Woodward's."

"That works," Tess said. "As I recall, they didn't sleep together in that movie. Just a lot of sexual tension."

"They were going to at the end," Nick said. "They were in the bedroom, laughing."

"They were getting married," Tess pointed out.

Nick parked the car beside Park's at the end of the lane. "Could work."

"What?"

Nick got out of the car and walked around to open her door, but she was already tripping out onto the gravel.

"I said, 'Could work,'" Nick repeated as he caught her upright.

"Getting married? Us? Are you nuts?"

"Yes," Nick said. "But it's situational madness. When I'm not around you, I'm a fully functioning adult. Don't worry. The urge will go away once I'm back in the city."

"Well, until then, try not to make any other insane suggestions," Tess said. "We're in public."

She jerked on the hem of her jacket and started up the steps.

"You know—" Nick began, but then the door opened, and he shut up in surprise. Tess looked up to find an aging monolith in a severe suit waiting placidly before her, backlit by the light from the hall. He looked like a cross between Abraham Lincoln and Lurch of the Addams Family.

"Hi," Tess said, holding out her hand. "I'm Tess Newhart."

"How do you do, Miss Newhart," the man said, nodding. "I am Henderson, Mr. Welch's manservant." He stepped back from the door, and Tess dropped her hand and stepped through, prodded from behind by Nick and the suitcase.

"If you'll follow me," Henderson said, "I will show you to your rooms. I hope you'll find your stay with us a most pleasant one."

"Oh, me, too," Tess said, and then winced as Nick bumped her with the suitcase to shut her up. "I didn't know people had menservants anymore," Tess whispered to Nick as they followed Henderson up the *Gone with the Wind* staircase. "Where do you suppose he got him? Sears?"

"Don't start," Nick said, and Tess laughed.

She laughed again once she was in her room and the door was shut behind her. The huge bedroom was papered in faded Early American blue and furnished in massive Early American walnut. The heavily carved bed was piled high with blue damask pillows that rose to within inches of a sampler that said Idle Hands Are the Devil's Playground.

Nick came through the connecting bathroom from his room to see what was so funny.

"Give the man credit for having a sense of humor." Tess gestured to the sampler. "What a thing to hang over a bed."

"You know," Nick said, looking at her appraisingly, "I have idle hands."

Tess frowned at him, mentally stomping on her traitorous thoughts about what those hands could do. "You have an idle mind. It's not the same thing."

"Well, come here and occupy both." Nick grinned at her, and Tess felt her breath catch. She backed up a step.

"I don't think so," she said.

Nick jerked his head toward the sampler. "It's the only moral thing to do. You wouldn't want me to end up as the Devil's playground, would you?"

"As far as I'm concerned, you already are the Devil's playground," Tess said. "I can't believe you're trying to seduce me with a sampler."

"I just think the idea deserves some serious consideration."

"Well, you'll have a lot of time to seriously consider it tonight," Tess said. "In your own bedroom. Go away."

THE BEFORE-DINNER PARTY was in full but dignified swing when Nick ushered a black-creped Tess into Welch's tastefully male living room an hour later. The place was a quietly ostentatious display of massive walnut furniture, coffee-colored leather, beige-striped walls and enough brass to outfit a band. Welch had decorated his house in money and leather and liquor cabinets and matched sets of never-opened calf-bound books, and then filled it with people with stiff upper lips who were dressed in clothes that were so well tailored they could probably stand without the people in them.

Tess felt herself stiffen and told herself to relax, shut up and make nice. It was only for two days, and she looked properly adult in her crepe dress, a dress that had been perfectly pressed by Henderson, who had appeared at her door to suggest that her clothes might have been mussed in the packing process. Henderson was so brilliant at this that he managed to make it sound as though the wrinkles were his fault, and Tess had handed over her dress because she couldn't bear to disappoint him by turning him down. Now he was quietly making sure that everyone found the buffet, had a full glass and wasn't lifting the silver. Watching Henderson alone might make up for the weekend, Tess thought as Nick led her across the lush carpet to the padded bar. It was so rare to see a man who simply took care of everything and then faded into the background. This must be why men liked having wives. Since she wasn't eligible for a wife, maybe someday she could have a Henderson. Maybe Nick would give her one for Christmas. It did seem mercenary of her, but she was prepared to share him with Gina. Gina would love having a Henderson.

Then she saw Gina standing at the bar, looking up at Park with her face glowing.

Not good.

"What's wrong?" Nick asked.

"Nothing," Tess said absently. Park must have turned on the charm on the drive down. She watched him with Gina for a moment and then tried to make herself be fair. He was smiling down at Gina, laughing with her, paying absolutely rapt attention to her. No wonder she was glowing. Still, there was no point in Gina's getting involved with Park. Park made movie stars look stable.

"That's Gina," Nick said, startled.

"Of course that's Gina," Tess said, still annoyed with Park. "You told me to get Park a date."

"I told you to get him a respectable date."

"Hey." Tess transferred her annoyance to Nick the lawyer. "That's my best friend you're trashing there. Back off."

"I like Gina," Nick said, and then looked back at the bar with a troubled face. "But frankly I don't think her grammar and her gum are up to this kind of party."

"She will do fine," Tess said coldly, and stomped toward the bar, enraged with Nick and with Park and with herself for getting Gina into this.

"Oh, great. Tess Trueheart in person," Park said when they reached them. "The sweetest girl in town." He looked at Nick. "I suppose you had to."

Tess's temper flared. This was the jerk who had lured Nick into yuppiedom, and now he was making fun of her. All the antagonism she'd felt for her landlord and the Foundation trustees and Nick fused into her glare at Park. "Great to see you, Park," she said. "Did I ever mention that your name sounds like low-income housing?"

"Tess," Gina said weakly.

"Still the same tact, I see," Park said, glaring back.

"Still the same tan, I see," Tess said. "You know, studies have shown that excessive tanning—"

"Gina, you look terrific," Nick said, kicking Tess smartly on the ankle.

"—can lead to skin cancer and premature aging," Tess said, moving out of his reach. "Just wanted you to know."

"Thank you," Park said. "I'm touched."

"Aw, Tess," Gina said.

"Come on, Tess," Nick muttered under his breath. "Play nice."

"He started it," Tess said.

"Oh, that's very mature," Nick said. "Could you please try and act like an adult?"

"Tess," Gina said pleadingly.

"Okay, okay. I'm sorry. Let's try this again." Tess took a deep breath and smiled a nice bright toothpaste smile. "Hello, Park, it's good to see you again."

Park smiled back tightly. "Always a pleasure, Tess."

"Now see," Nick said, "that wasn't so hard, was it?"

Tess shot him a look of contempt and took Gina's arm. "I need to talk to you," she whispered before she turned to Park and Nick and said, "Gina and I are going to go find the ladies' room to freshen our lipstick."

All three of them looked at her with varying degrees of surprise.

"All right," Tess said. "Gina will freshen hers, and I'll put some on."

"Right," Gina said, gamely picking up her cue. "That would be good."

Tess pulled Gina up the stairs to the master bathroom in search of privacy. When the door was shut behind them, she turned to Gina. "I'm worried about you. It would be a bad idea to get hung up on Park."

"Look at this bathroom." Gina drifted past the walls covered in mint green hand-painted tiles to stroke the porcelain of the huge pale green tub. "I don't think I've ever seen tile without mildew before. This is so *beautiful*."

Tess ducked under one of the dozen ferns that was suspended from the ceiling and looked around, annoyed. "If this is what the rain forest looks like, I'm going to stop trying to save it."

"Oh, Tess." Gina sank into the rattan chair beside the tub. "Admit it. This is paradise."

"No, it isn't. You're just confused because of the vegetation. This is merely an extremely pretentious bathroom. I bet Norbert Welch wears a sarong when he's in here. No, that's not right. Guys don't wear sarongs. A loincloth." She thought about Welch as she'd seen him pictured on the back of his last book, short, hefty and sullen, only this time in a loincloth. "Maybe not."

"I don't mean just the bathtub," Gina said. "I mean everything. Everything about the way these people live. Park took me out for a drink before we left. At The Levee." Her voice fell, hushed, on the last word.

"I've been," Tess said, nodding. "Nick took me once. Overpriced food, obsequious waiters and really good wine. If they'd put in a drive-through, I'd consider going back for the wine."

"It was so beautiful," Gina went on, not hearing her. "And everybody was so nice and there weren't any prices on the menu."

"If you have to ask, you can't afford it," Tess said. "And they weren't nice. They were sucking up. If you were a nobody, they'd have spat on you."

"Well, that's the point," Gina said. "I am a nobody. But when I'm with Park, I'm somebody."

"This conversation is taking an ugly turn," Tess said sternly. "You are *not* a nobody."

Gina sank back slowly in the chair, drawing her fingers back and forth across the flawless porcelain of the tub next to her as she spoke. "Ever since Park picked me up, I haven't worried about anything. I know the car's not gonna break down, that there's gonna be enough money to pay for the drinks, that Park's not gonna wrestle me down on the car seat, and that it doesn't matter that my step-ball-change is not as good as it used to be."

"Don't bet on the Park-and-the-car-seat part," Tess said, but she sounded distracted. She slid her spine down the bathroom door and sat up on the floor, trying not to tear the seams out of her crepe dress. "Are you still serious about giving up your dancing?"

"Yes." Gina met Tess's eyes. "I'm done. I'm tired and I hurt. I've always hurt, every dancer hurts, but somehow it hurts more now. I want to settle down and find a nice job in the theater selling tickets or something, and then find a nice man and have some kids and a real life."

Tess leaned her head back against the door and closed her eyes. "Tell me you're not thinking of Park as a nice man."

"Listen." Gina leaned forward. "I know that marrying Park is not for me. But he is a nice man. And he's treated me like a queen all night. I've never been out with anybody like him."

"I can believe that," Tess said. "There is nobody like him. He's Andrew Dice Clay with breeding."

"No, he's not," Gina insisted. "He's *nice*. He's a good person. I *like* him."

"Fine." Tess held up her hands in alarm. "Fine. Just don't get serious about him. Don't count on him."

Gina laughed mirthlessly. "Oh, I'm not. I know he's not my future. In fact, I'm working on my future. The Charles Theater needs a secretary. I've got an interview Monday afternoon."

"A secretary?" Tess had a vivid, horrific vision of Gina chained to a typewriter. "You can't type. Think of something else."

Gina slumped back in her chair again. "Could you just once be supportive?"

"I'm sorry," Tess said, appalled at the look on her friend's face. "I'm really sorry. I think you'd make a fantastic addition to any theater. I think you'd be the best thing that ever happened to Park. I think you're the best friend I've ever had, and I'm really sorry I've been such a bummer here. Give me a minute and I'll be supportive. I just wasn't thinking."

"You don't need a minute," Gina said gloomily. "Park is probably already looking for another woman, and you're right, I can't type."

Tess shook her head, scrambling through her thoughts to find something positive. "That doesn't matter. You know the theater better than any secretary could possibly know it. And you know theater people. They'd be crazy not to snap you up as some kind of administrative assistant. And I think you should tell them that." Tess warmed to her subject. "They'd be crazy to waste you typing and filing. Tell them everything you've done, everything you know, tell them—"

"Tess . . ."

Tess stopped.

"It's okay," Gina said. "The job part isn't that big a deal. But please, let me have this weekend with Park without making any snotty cracks."

Tess swallowed. "You've got it."

"Thank you." Gina bit her lip.

Tess blinked back tears that had somehow formed when she wasn't paying attention. "But if he's not good to you, I will take him apart."

"He's good to me," Gina said. "He's really good to me. He told me I was the nicest person he'd ever dated and that I make him laugh and that I'm beautiful. He thinks I'm beautiful."

"You are beautiful."

"I look Italian," Gina said.

"You are Italian," Tess said, confused. "Beautifully Italian."

"I know," Gina said, exasperated. "But Park is probably one of those guys who only dates WASPs. WASPs with college educations and ivy growing on them. And he thinks I'm beautiful."

"Well, hell, he should," Tess said. "Even I don't think Park's such a snob that he'd only date Ivy League blondes."

"You don't understand," Gina said. "I never even graduated from high school, and he still listens to me. He's wonderful."

"I don't think education is a big criteria for Park's dates," Tess said. "And who cares whether you graduated or not? You're still a great person and you've been everywhere and you know a hell of a lot about the world. Of course he listens to you."

"You don't understand," Gina said hopelessly.

"All right," Tess said, but she had a sinking feeling that she did understand, only too well. Gina had fallen for Park and it was all her fault. She'd fixed them up. *Good job, Tess,* she told herself, and then shook her head when Gina frowned at her. "All right," she said again. "I'm with you on this."

"Good." Gina swallowed nervously. "Do you think it would be okay if I had some gum?"

"No," Tess said. "But what the hell, chew it, anyway."

"No," Gina said. "I'm not gonna embarrass Park. If you see me doing anything dumb, stop me."

"Don't change for him," Tess insisted, appalled. "Don't do it. You're a great person."

"Just for the weekend," Gina said. "Just for this weekend."

"LONG TIME in the bathroom," Nick said when they went back to the party, but he was smiling at her as if he'd missed her, and she felt pleased and then immediately kicked herself for feeling pleased. Big deal, he'd missed her. So what. Then he put his arm around her, and she forgot Gina and her problems for a moment and just enjoyed the weight and warmth of his arm on her back and the pleasure of being with him again. *Steady,* she told herself, trying hard not to lean into him. *Get through this weekend and get out, because this man is not for you. He has bad values and worse ambitions. Remember that.*

But all she said was, "We got lost in the ferns. They should hand out machetes at the door."

"Well, don't disappear again," Nick said. "We're going in to dinner soon." Then he leaned over and whispered in her ear, "There are two Decker board members here. Watch your step, don't say *anything* controversial and smile at everybody."

"Who are the board members?" Tess whispered back.

"Annalise Donaldson and Robert Tyler." Nick nodded toward a portly gray-haired man on the other side of the room. "That's Tyler. I haven't seen Donaldson yet, but she's here. Welch said so."

"Donaldson, Tyler," Tess said. "She collects terra-cotta, he's a big Bengals fan."

Nick raised an eyebrow. "And how do we know this?"

"We did our research," Tess said. "Lead me to 'em. I'm ready."

"Dinner is served," Henderson announced.

Welch had evidently given up his lust for leather in the dining room, but the same giant walnut furniture prevailed and the same beige paper striped the walls. Tess speculated that maybe he'd gotten a deal from a walnut-and-wallpaper place, but before she could share her theory with Nick, Henderson showed them to their seats. Tess was next to Norbert Welch at the head of the table with Nick on her right and Park and Gina across the table from them, one seat down. An attractive blond woman came to take the chair between Welch and Park.

"So this is the little woman," Welch said to Nick as they reached the table, and Tess turned to look at him in disbelief. Nobody in her life had ever called her a little woman.

For a great American author, he was a lot younger and a lot shorter than she'd expected, even after seeing his photo on the book jacket. He couldn't be past his early fifties and his eyes were a couple of inches below hers, which meant he was five six at most. But his face lived up to legend. He looked like a macho literary lion: his thick mane of white hair was so long it covered his ears and then waved back from his battered, square-jawed face, a weathered prize-fighter kind of face that was etched with a permanent scowl. He was the only person in the room who didn't look as if he'd been designed to go with the decor.

Tess blinked when she realized that he was studying her as closely as she was studying him.

"Good to see you again, sir," Nick said as he reached across Tess to shake Welch's hand. "I don't believe you've met my fiancée, Tess Newhart."

"I don't believe I have," Welch rumbled. "So you're the future Mrs. Jamieson."

Tess resisted the urge to explain that she'd be keeping her maiden name, since the point was moot, given that she wasn't marrying Nick. She smiled instead and heard Nick give a very small sigh of relief next to her. "That's me. Thank you for inviting us to your home. We're enjoying ourselves tremendously. And I can't wait to hear your new book. Henderson told us earlier that you're reading from it tomorrow." She started to ask him where he'd bought Henderson and if they took MasterCard, but Welch overrode her.

"I bet you can't wait," Welch said. "The question is, have you read any of my other books? Or are you waiting for the movies?"

"Oh, I've read them all," Tess said. "I was assigned *The Last Promise* in college, and then read the other two on my own. Of course that was many years ago. How long has it been since *Disenchanted Evenings?* Fifteen years?"

"Why don't you sit down now, Tess?" Nick said to her grimly, pulling out her chair for her. "And remember where you are."

"Back off, Jamieson," Welch snapped at him. "When I can't take it, I'll let you know."

"Actually I really am looking forward to hearing you read," Tess said, sinking into her chair.

"Because you're so taken with my philosophy?" Welch asked, baiting her.

"No, I'm not crazy about your philosophy," Tess said. "I just like your writing."

She smiled at him cheerfully, and Welch blinked in disgruntled surprise. "Thank you."

"You're welcome," Tess said. "Your house is nice, too. Did you pick out the sampler in my bedroom?"

Welch snorted with laughter. "You liked that, did you?"

"Loved it," Tess said.

Welch laughed again and then turned to the woman on his left. "You should see this sampler, Tricia," he said to her, and she cooed at him, practically consuming him with obvious celebrity-collector's greed.

"Who's she?" Tess asked Nick when Welch turned away and Henderson began to serve.

"This is a good sign," Nick murmured at the same time, not hearing her question. "He's taking me pretty seriously to sit us here. But, God, Tess, watch your mouth. Don't blow this for me."

"I think he likes it when I talk back," Tess said, but then she was distracted by Henderson. "I want one of those," she whispered to Nick.

"What would you do with him if you had him?" Nick whispered back. "Staple signs to him for demonstrations?"

Tess sighed. "I just like the way he controls the universe. You know, before dinner somebody was saying that he even watches what Welch eats because he has a heart condition. Welch doesn't even have to do his own dieting. Henderson sees to it." She shook her head in admiration. "It would be really nice to have a man around to take care of me like that."

"Hey." Nick pointed to his chest. "Let's not forget the obvious here. What about me?"

She looked at him, warm and broad and smiling next to her, and thought, *anytime*, but all she said was, "You're cute, but you're not Henderson."

"Hey," Nick said again, but then Henderson began to serve, and Tess minded her manners beautifully through most of the entrée.

Then Welch pushed his plate back and said, "So, Miss Newhart," and Tess looked at him inquiringly.

"You say you're not crazy about my philosophy," Welch went on. "Now your philosophy would be what, exactly?" He looked at her from under his brows, and Tess saw a definite challenge there.

Be good, she reminded herself. *This is important for Nick.* "My philosophy is to behave myself so I get invited back for dinner again," she told him. "This is excellent beef. Does Henderson do your cooking?"

"Yes," Welch said, "and you're ducking the question."

"Well, I'm trying to behave," Tess said. "It's always a struggle for me. Now where exactly did you get Hen—"

"The hell with behaving," Welch said. "Show a little spirit. I know you're under Jamieson's thumb here, but you must have some ideas of your own."

Tess held back the first dozen retorts that occurred to her. "Can't think of one," she said. "You know us women. Short on philosophy, long on shopping."

"Didn't pick this one for her brains, did you, Jamieson?" Welch said, but he kept his eyes on Tess.

"Tess is brilliant—" Nick began quietly, but Tess waved him silent.

"What are you up to?" she asked Welch, and was rewarded with a grin. "I thought so. You're just trying to get me in trouble. Well, forget it. Pass the butter. Did Henderson bake these rolls, too?"

"A woman without a philosophy," Welch said, passing her the butter dish. "Why am I not surprised?"

"All right, all right, I have a philosophy," Tess said, trying to play the game for Nick's sake. "Well, it's not really mine. It's one I borrowed. I had a friend a very long time ago who used to say that the only way to live life was to look for the best in every day and make sure I had a part in creating some of it. That still works for me."

"Oh, Lord," Park groaned.

"How charming," the blond woman across from Tess said, making it obvious that she didn't think so.

"I think it is," Gina said, a truly brave act since she'd been silent, staring at her plate, ever since they'd all sat down.

Tess turned to her, smiling, but Welch was already on the attack. "Sounds like sixties' garbage."

Tess swung back to him, and then she felt Nick's hand grip her thigh. *Don't say anything*, she thought, and then she nodded a little, and Nick moved his hand away.

The blond woman tittered. "Oh, Norbert."

Encouraged, Welch went on. "You're probably one of those fools who thinks literature should be life-affirming."

Tess frowned at him and opened her mouth, but Nick's hand was back before she could speak. "Tess teaches literature," he said. "I'm sure she has many interesting theories about it, but right now—"

Welch interrupted him. "So now you're the spokesman for her? What happened to her mouth?"

"Spokesperson," Tess said. "And my mouth is right here. Biding its time."

"Spokesperson?" Park said, confused.

"Nongender-specific term." Tess watched Welch grow red with annoyance and smiled cheerfully at him in response.

He caught her grin and stopped scowling, nodding at her slightly to acknowledge the hit. "Politically correct garbage," he said, baiting her again. "Stupid words."

"Definitely," the blonde agreed, totally oblivious to the byplay going on in front of her.

"Patriarchy is dead, folks." Tess beamed at them both. "Get used to it."

The pressure from Nick's hand on her thigh increased to the point of pain.

"The hell it is," Welch grumped. "Not in my house."

Tess laughed at Welch, at the same time attempting to move her leg out of Nick's grip. "What are you trying to do? Recapture the fifties?"

Welch snorted at her again. "Makes more sense than reliving the sixties. 'Course, you're a real radical, probably protesting all over the place." He shook his head at her, obviously fighting back a grin as he looked at her from under his brows, his head lowered like a bull ready to charge. "You really think that crap does any good?"

Tess felt her temper flare and stomped on it. Getting mad was what Welch wanted her to do, the old goat. If she wanted to help Nick, the best thing she could do was shut up.

She shut up.

Nick moved his hand away again, patting her knee in gratitude as he did so.

Welch needled her some more. "Your problem is that you're in the wrong decade. The hippies are gone, Tess. Give it up."

"Give it up?" Tess said, holding on to her temper. "Then who will do it if I don't?"

"That's what I thought—you're a martyr. And for what? All that protesting never accomplished squat, anyway." Welch grinned at her. "Sixties' stuff. That's all out of date now."

"Well, *values* are timeless," Tess said goaded beyond endurance. "Do you have any?"

"How about this roast beef?" Nick said. "And the gravy? My compliments to the cook."

"Butt out, Jamieson," Welch said, and then went back on attack. "Yeah, I have values. Hard work, drive and success. Those are my values. And they'll get me a lot farther than your touchy-feely ideals will get you." He peered at her, watching avidly for her reaction, but Tess was suddenly too angry to notice.

"Values aren't buses," she said shortly. "They're not supposed to get you anywhere. They're supposed to define who you are. And I'd rather be touchy-feely than morally bankrupt."

"Well, really," the blonde said.

"Awfully nice party," Park said.

"Well, I'd rather be morally bankrupt than literally bankrupt," Welch shot back. "Right, Jamieson?"

They both turned to Nick.

"I'd rather not be either," Nick said. "I'm certainly looking forward to hearing you read tomorrow, sir."

Welch closed his eyes in disgust. "Typical lawyer."

"On that we agree," Tess said, and was surprised to see him grin at her.

"Good for you," Welch said, and turned back to the blonde, laughing, and began to talk to her.

"What was that all about?" Tess asked Nick.

"That was the sound of one account escaping," Park hissed at her across the table, glaring.

"Oh, no," Gina said, and absentmindedly began to eat faster in distress.

"Will you please shut up for the rest of the night?" Park continued. "I know you won't do it for me, but think of Nick for a change."

Tess met Nick's eyes.

"Just eat," Nick said, and Tess picked up her fork and looked across the table in time to see Gina sopping up the last of her gravy with a roll. She tried to catch her eye to shake her head, but Gina was oblivious in her tension. *That's my fault, too*, Tess thought, and tried to kick her friend under the table, but she caught Park instead.

He turned outraged eyes on her just as the blonde said, "My dear, what *are* you doing?" to Gina.

Gina froze, roll in hand.

"She's making the most of this delicious gravy," Tess said with a pointed glare at the blonde who glared back. Tess picked up her roll to do the same, perfectly prepared to filet the blonde if she said one more word to Gina.

"Well, really," the blonde said again, and Tess opened her mouth but Nick was already speaking.

"It's the only way," Nick agreed instantly and picked up his own roll. "Don't you think, Park?"

Park was still looking at Gina's plate in puzzlement, but he caught on gamely. "Absolutely," he said, looking around the table for a roll.

"Oh, no," Gina said faintly, dropping hers.

"She's right," Welch said from the end of the table. "Good for you, kid. I like a woman who knows how to eat."

Gina's smile was so weak it barely existed.

The blonde looked up from the bread on her plate to glare at Tess, clearly not sure where she stood on the roll question but definitely sure where she stood on Tess.

Tess ignored her and turned back to Welch. "I like you," she said. "I apologize for the morally bankrupt part."

Welch grinned at her, and she felt Nick relax with a sigh beside her and begin to speak to the blonde across the table, smoothing her ruffled feelings as only Nick the snake-oil salesman could.

Tess leaned toward Welch. "You know, I didn't get that woman's name," she whispered to him. "Who is she?"

Welch lowered his voice so the blonde wouldn't hear him. "Tricia Sigler."

"Sigler?" Tess said, taken aback.

"Yeah," Welch said, watching with interest.

Tess felt her stomach sinking. "Any relation to Alan Sigler? The Decker Academy?"

"Husband. He couldn't make it tonight. She came alone." Welch looked at her with calculation. "What's the Decker Academy to you?"

"I was thinking about getting a job there," Tess said. She felt like kicking herself. Nick had warned her. Gina had warned her. Hell, even Park had warned her. It was her own fault that she'd antagonized the wife of the only ally she had at Decker. Dumb. She sighed and then realized Welch was watching her and smiled brightly at him to distract him. "So tell me," she said, "exactly where did you get Henderson? My first thought was Sears, but after watching him in action, I've switched my guess to Nieman Marcus."

Welch's roar of laughter beautifully covered Nick's groan, but it didn't do anything to dim Tricia Sigler's basilisk glare.

5

TWO HOURS LATER, Nick stood in the doorway to Tess's bedroom in his pajama bottoms and tried to forget the dozen different times during the evening that Tess had teased Welch with animated banter, and the way Welch's eyes had followed her around the room even when she wasn't saying something outrageous to him. It would be ridiculous and petty of him to be jealous of Welch. He should be grateful to Tess for so obviously captivating the man, but every time he thought of Welch growling at her in evident appreciation, it was hard to remember why he wanted the contract, or why he wanted anyone as undignified as Tess, especially since she had now draped herself in about thirty yards of pink-flowered flannel nightgown and was sitting on the bed watching him warily.

"This is not how I'd pictured this night," he said.

"Oh? And how had you pictured it?"

"Well, to begin with, you weren't wearing flannel," Nick said. "But forget that for now. Did you have to argue with Welch the entire night?"

"He started it," Tess said. "And besides, I think he liked it. You know, I don't think he's healthy." She frowned as her train of thought switched tracks. "I don't think this dieting is enough. Maybe I should say something to Henderson about cutting off his booze, too."

"No," Nick said, moving toward her. "Absolutely not. You will not say anything to Henderson."

"Well, not tonight, anyway." Tess crawled into bed and flapped her hand at him. "You may go now. I've got a big day of fighting with Welch tomorrow, and then there's the reading in the afternoon. I need my sleep." She slumped down under the covers and switched off the bedside light, and then she turned her back to him.

"Right." Nick sat on the bed and switched the light back on. "Come on, Tess. We need to talk."

WHEN HE SAT next to her on the bed, Tess debated ignoring him, but knowing Nick, he wouldn't quit. He leaned on the pillow next to her, and she rolled over to talk to him and then regretted it.

His arms were even better close up than she remembered, the swell of his bicep neatly cleaving into the long lovely line of his shoulder, the hint of his tricep promising—

She rolled away from him, trying to get her breath back, vaguely wondering why, for her, it had always been arms, and why he had to have such great ones.

"Tess?"

"Go to sleep."

"I think we should talk."

"Go to sleep."

"I mean it," Nick insisted over her shoulder. "We have a lot of history that needs sorting out. You're still mad about that parking-lot thing. I'm still confused about why you won't go out with me. I think—"

Tess rolled over and ended up against his chest. "You necked with me in a parking lot until I was insane with lust and then you said you didn't want to sleep with me, but you don't know why I won't go out with you? And just for the record, I'm spending the *weekend* with you, so don't try that just-give-me-a-chance garbage on me. I'm helping you, you ingrate."

"See, I think we should talk," Nick said, and she was momentarily distracted by the backlighting on his deltoid and how warm his chest was against her cheek, and her breath went again.

"Put on a shirt, and we'll talk," Tess said and rolled away from him again.

"Fine."

She felt Nick get off the bed, then come back a few moments later. She checked over her shoulder. The shirt was on. It wasn't buttoned, and he did have a nice chest. Well, actually he had a great chest, but chests were resistible. It was arms that made her weak. "Okay," she said, sitting up in bed and propping a pillow against the headboard behind her. "Talk."

He propped the other pillow next to hers and relaxed against it. "Let's get the worst over with first. The parking lot."

"Good choice." Tess seized on past anger to defuse present desire. "I am definitely still hostile about that damn parking lot."

"Well, first, I *never* said I didn't want to sleep with you—" Nick began.

"You said no."

"I said I didn't want to make love with you in the front seat of my car in the middle of the Music Hall parking lot because, among other things, it's against the damn law." He glared at her.

Tess glared back. "*This* is an apology?"

"No," Nick said. "This is an explanation. I was more than willing, perfectly willing, extremely willing, to take you back to my apartment and make love with you all night if necessary, but you got all huffy—"

"What's romantic about going back to your apartment?" Tess asked him, annoyed.

"What's romantic about doing it in the front seat of a sports car?" Nick retaliated. "Hell, I'm not even sure it's possible. There's not that much room."

"We could have found out," Tess said. "But no, you had to be respectable and responsible—"

"Besides, I have a career on the line here—"

"—and dull and boring—"

"—which I realize means nothing to you—"

"—and *completely* unexciting—"

"—but it means a lot to me—"

"—not to mention a grave comment on how little you actually wanted me—"

"—or at least enough that I'm not going to risk it for sex in a car—"

"—which is why I see no reason in pursuing this relationship—"

"—and anyway I prefer beds—"

"—so you can just go back to your own bed!" Tess flared.

"—like this one, for example," Nick finished.

"What?"

"I think we should make love," Nick said.

Tess looked at him incredulously. "Did you hear a word I just said?"

"No. I was explaining my point. What did you say?"

"Get out of my bed," Tess ordered.

"Why? I just apologized."

"No, you didn't," Tess said. "You were explaining something to me about your career. That's not an apology. That's a red flag. In fact, if you ever want to start a fight with me, mention how much more important your career is to you than I am. Trust me, it'll work every time."

Nick blinked. "Let me try again. I'm sorry if I hurt your feelings that night in the parking lot. I didn't say no because I didn't want you. I said no because of where we were. I know you'll never understand that, but at least believe me when I say it wasn't you."

Tess looked up into his face and thought about how sweet he could be and how great his lips felt on hers and how good it would feel to be wrapped around him and how hot she would be if she rolled against him and how she was going to start screaming pretty soon if she didn't have him, and her anger evaporated. She sank back against the pillow, trying hard not to surrender. "All right. I still don't agree with you, but I believe you, and I may have overreacted, so I'll take part of the responsibility. You're forgiven. You can go now."

"May have overreacted?" Nick said. "You didn't talk to me for six weeks because I said, 'Let's wait fifteen minutes,' but you only may have overreacted?"

"Do you want to fight about that, too?" Tess asked.

"No," Nick said, backtracking. "I don't want to fight about anything."

Tess leaned back against her pillow and tried to think of something else to fight with him about while she watched him from under her lashes. The problem with Nick was that, aside from the fact that she never knew when he was going to be Alan Alda and when he was going to be Donald Trump, it was getting harder and harder to pick a fight with him because he was right there in bed with her, and if she reached out she could have him, and she wanted him.

She really wanted him.

Getting involved with somebody like Nick was such a bad idea. He'd get mad at the things she did; she'd get hurt because he wanted a partnership more than her. She'd forget to protect his career; he'd forget her name in pursuit of it. The whole idea had Doomed written all over it.

She could see the line of his shoulder through the pajama top, which he still hadn't buttoned. His neck curved cleanly down into his shoulder, his pectorals swelled and then flattened into the abdominals across his stomach, his biceps bulged because his arms were crossed . . .

Nick reached across and gently brushed a strand of her hair from her eyes with his finger. "Come on, Tess. What else do you want to throw at me?"

"Thank you for introducing me to all those people tonight," she said, trying to keep the lust from her voice.

He blinked in surprise. "You came here to help me. You don't owe me anything for helping you back. Besides, I want you to get the Decker job."

"You know, just when I think you're a valueless twit, you do something nice for me," Tess said. "Like when you came downtown to the police station in the middle of the night last month."

"Oh, that was because you'd been arrested for soliciting." Nick relaxed against the pillow, his cheek close to hers, and moved his hand into the curve of her waist. Tess bit her lip so she wouldn't moan. "I thought you'd taken to the streets. I had a hundred bucks ready."

"Very funny." Tess shifted a little and felt his hand tighten on her, and her thoughts drifted off momentarily into a sea of lust. Then she yanked her mind back to what they were talking about. "And you know very well I wasn't arrested for soliciting."

"Well, I was hoping." Nick slid his arm across her waist and pulled her a little closer. "I liked that story a lot better than the one about you taking pictures of johns' license plates to stop prostitution in your neighborhood." He brushed a kiss against her forehead.

"It was a good idea," Tess said, trying to ignore him and failing miserably. Despite her better judgment, she snuggled against him.

"No, it wasn't." Nick moved even closer, and she felt the lovely long length of his body warm hers and the heat turned her brain to mush. "But I don't care enough about this one to argue," he finished.

"I don't, either," Tess said, fighting for coherence. "What have we got left to fight about?"

"As long as we stay away from politics, nothing," Nick said, hope making his voice light. "The parking lot's not an issue anymore, right?"

"Right," Tess said. "Guess we'll have to fight about politics."

"Why?" Nick kissed her cheek, moving closer to her mouth. "Why can't we just get along?"

Tess slumped down farther in the bed and shut her eyes tight so she couldn't see his mouth and be tempted by it. "Because if we get along, I'll end up sleeping with you," she said, her own mouth partially under the covers. "I can't handle that."

"Wait a minute." Nick pulled back and shot her an outraged look. "You start fights so we won't have sex?"

"Not always," Tess said, both relieved and disappointed that he was farther away. Her voice began to rise as she fought not to reach out to him. "Sometimes you're such a yuppie I have to fight with you. But a lot of the time, yes—because you really are a good person and you really do turn me on, and God knows I want you, but I know it's no good because you do things like make snide cracks about Gina and all you think about is that damn law firm, so I just keep telling myself what a throwback you are even if you are being darling at the moment, and how if I give in to you I'll end up barefoot and pregnant in a shirtwaist reading Marabel Morgan and wearing my hair in a Marilyn Quayle flip while you work late at the office! I can't stand it! I just can't trust you! You're like Jekyll and Hyde." She sat up suddenly and glared at him, crazed with lust and anger. "And I've got to tell you," she spat at him, "I really *hate* Jekyll."

"Jekyll was the *good* guy," Nick said through his teeth, and then he sat up and rested his arms on his knees, looking away from her and controlling his temper with obvious effort.

"No, Jekyll was the *conservative* guy," Tess said. "He always did the correct thing and he never had any emotions and all he cared about was public opinion."

"Hyde beat an old guy to death with a stick," Nick said, turning to glare at her. "This is what you want me to be?"

"Actually I always thought that part was sexually significant," Tess said, momentarily distracted. "But, no, of course not. I just want you to have an emotion that hasn't been previously approved by the Opera Guild and seven area churches."

"You are exaggerating."

"Oh?" Tess leaned back against the headboard and folded her arms. "Well, then why didn't you make love to me at the Music Hall?"

"I thought we settled this already. It was a parking lot," Nick said. "Public indecency is a misdemeanor."

"Thank you, Dr. Jekyll," Tess said. "I rest my case."

Nick closed his eyes for a moment, and Tess waited for him to get out of the bed, go in his room and slam the door behind him. The disappointment that thought engendered made her weak. She didn't want him going back to his bedroom. She wanted him coming inside her. And if she wanted him that much, maybe it was time to stop saying no. Maybe—

"Tell me something," Nick said suddenly, rolling next to her so he was leaning over her. "Why did you agree to come this weekend, and why are you in bed with me, knowing as you must have that this would come up?"

"I came this weekend because I really want the Decker job," Tess said, and then she slid a little lower on the pillows to peer up at him. "But I'm in this bed with you because I really want you. I guess I was hoping you'd sweep me off my feet."

"Well, hell, I'm *trying* to," Nick said. "You want to give me a few pointers?"

"No," Tess said, but he was so close and she wanted his mouth on hers and his arms around her, and the more she thought about it, the more she wanted him, and it was taking everything she had not to just pull him down to her and kiss him. *Think of something else,* she thought, and then she looked into his eyes and knew that she wasn't going to think of anything else and that she was definitely going to make love with him that night.

And so she pulled him down to her and kissed him.

ANY LINGERING QUESTIONS Nick might have had as to why he was wasting his time on a bleeding-heart liberal flake disappeared when Tess kissed him. He'd been waiting for her for a year without realizing it—ever since she'd sobbed in his arms about breaking up with her latest loser, warm and round and vulnerable and still fighting mad, apologizing for crying on his shirt and then curling up against him to sob again, so nakedly emotional that he'd been blown wide open by the experience. He'd been telling himself ever since that his attraction to her was just sexual, but the relief he felt when she finally kissed him was a lot more than just pleasure that he was finally going to have her body. He realized with a sinking heart what he'd known all along and had preferred to ignore—his feelings for Tess weren't just about sex.

It was possibly the worst revelation he'd ever had.

Then Tess traced his lips with her tongue and arched her body up to meet his, and he felt the bed move beneath him as he slid his arms around her and pulled her close.

No, this wasn't just about sex, but for the next hour or so, it was going to be mostly about sex.

Her mouth was hot and tasted of peppermint and salt and Tess, and he lingered there, tasting her, because she was like no one else he'd ever kissed. And then she sat up and pushed him away gently, and he braced himself for an argument on Republican kissing. But she only pulled her nightgown over her head, yards of flannel flowing past his face, releasing her scent, and then she threw the gown on the floor by the bed, and he watched her stretch in the lamplight, her breasts round and full above the slope of her stomach. Without thinking, he said, "Park was right."

Tess stopped. "What?"

"Forget it." Nick stripped off his shirt and reached for her, shaking slightly as her skin touched his. Then he pulled her down on top of him to feel the soft weight of her on his chest. "God, you feel wonderful."

She kissed him again, biting his lip, and he lost himself in her heat, trailing his hand solidly down the curve of her back, pulling her hips tight against his and then rolling her under him, all without losing her mouth.

All he lost was his mind.

NICK WAS EVERYTHING Tess craved, all that solidity and security and excitement in one broad body pulsing against her. His weight anchored her as her mind moved into instinct and heat. Her fingers traced the corded lines of his back, her lips touched all the warm places she'd promised herself but never tasted. She shuddered under his hands, feeling soft and liquid against his hard heat, loving the way her body pressed against his, feeling every difference between them, hard and soft, rough and smooth, salt and sweet, until they rolled together, laughing and trembling at the desire that was driving them together. And because it was Nick, everything was easy and safe; the condom was in his pajama pocket, and then on

Nick, and then pressed against her, and she moved against him, grateful for his care and crazy for his touch.

And then Nick smiled at her, a smile that was lazy and thick with lust, and whispered, "Now," and pulled her hips to his, and she arched to meet him, and the shock of him moving inside her made her clutch at him while he moaned into her throat, and she relished the way he filled her until her eyes lost their focus. Then they weren't playing anymore; there was too much need. And Tess wrapped herself around him, trying to rock away the sudden mind-bending craving, scraping her fingernails down his back, biting into his shoulder as he surged hard against her, until finally the twisting hunger came welling up in her and she cried out. He muffled her mouth with his, pounding against her, inside her, leaving her mindless. And then they both lay shuddering together, twisted in the sheets, silenced by the shock of their coupling.

And when Nick finally moved away from her, Tess's sigh was more of a laugh, and he gathered her back close and kissed her, and she fell asleep, cradled against his chest.

6

EARLY THE NEXT MORNING, Tess sat on Welch's whitewashed pasture fence a hundred yards from the mansion's front door and brooded. She pulled her navy jacket closer around her and looked out at the rolling landscape: long-muscled horses, lush emerald green grass, a sky too blue to be real, all caressed by a gentle breeze perfumed with honeysuckle.

Bah humbug, she thought. *And those damn birds can shut up, too.*

"You look like hell this morning," Gina said from behind her, and Tess jerked in surprise, grabbing the fence post to keep from falling off. She frowned down at her friend, and Gina, swathed in a bulky black turtleneck, leaned against the fence, her face a mask of gloom. "If you're thinking about ending it all, wait—'cause I'm gonna go with you."

"Don't joke," Tess said. "It's a thought."

"I know why I'm depressed," Gina said. "I embarrassed myself and Park to pieces last night, and now I'm never gonna see him again, which I knew, anyway, but I still kinda had hopes. You know? Oh, hell." Gina climbed onto the fence beside Tess and twined her black-clad legs around the fence rails. "Why are you so upset? You and Nick have a fight?"

"No," Tess said gloomily. "We made love. It was wonderful. Then I woke up and he was gone. But he left a note." She fished a piece of paper out of her jacket pocket and handed it to Gina.

"'Gone to see Welch about the contract,'" Gina read. "'Things look good. See you at lunch. Nick.'" She frowned at Tess. "Are you sure you made love? 'Cause if you did, I don't think he remembers it."

"Well, I thought so." Tess sighed. "But I must have been wrong. And I was feeling so warm about him, too." She kicked her heel against the fence as she remembered. "I was all soft and squishy about it. And then he drops me a line as he leaves. He didn't even wake me up to kiss me. The *contract* comes first." She exhaled a long depressed breath. "I can't believe I fell for him again. It's not as if I didn't *know* he was like this. So I came out here to forget." She looked at Gina for the first time. "But I'll live. How about you? Did Park stop by your room to say good-night?"

"Yeah," Gina said. "And then he left."

"Really?" Tess blinked in surprise. "That seems unlike him. Maybe he respects you too much to make a move."

"Are you making fun?" Gina demanded. "You know why he didn't try anything. It was that thing I did with the gravy. I embarrassed him." She let her head drop lower. "I didn't know you weren't supposed to do that."

"No." Tess shook her head. "It wasn't that. He was surprised, but he didn't care." Gina groaned, and Tess shook her head again. "Stop it. It was no big deal. He didn't care. Nobody cared except that obnoxious Sigler woman." She winced as she thought about Tricia Sigler and her now even-more-distant chances for a job at Decker. Then with an effort she dragged her mind back to comforting Gina. "And I'm serious about the respect part. You were right about the way he treats you. I watched him all last night—ready to kill him if he snubbed you—but you were right. He does treat you like a queen. I've never seen him act like that with any other woman. So I think you're all right." Tess stopped to consider what she'd said. "If being involved with Park could ever be termed all right."

"Aw, Tess," Gina began.

Tess held up her hand. "Okay, okay. Enough of this obsessing about men. We knew they were rats to begin with. We're liberated women. We don't need them, anyway. Let's forget them and go get some breakfast." Tess climbed off the fence and started to stride away, and Gina dropped off and followed her, walking double time to keep up.

"You really think Park didn't care?" Gina asked, the pleading clear in her voice. "You really think he's different with me?"

"Yes," Tess said reluctantly. "Don't get me wrong, he's always been impeccably polite to every woman he's ever been with, but they've always been more—"

"Upper class," Gina said.

"—like accessories," Tess finished. "I swear, he picked some of them to go with his ties. But he talks to you. He listens to you. If you seem uncertain, he takes your hand. So maybe the reason he's not making a pass really is that he has too much respect for you."

Gina kicked the ground. "I don't want that much respect."

Tess sighed with exasperation. "Well, then, *do* something about it."

"What'd you do to get Nick to come across?"

"I breathed," Tess said glumly. "Nick's a self-starter. And when he's done, evidently he's done. I should have known."

Gina shrugged. "So don't see him again after this weekend."

"Oh, I'm not going to, but . . ." Tess stopped walking, concentrating on trying to put her unhappiness into words. "I'll miss him. The good Nick. I'll miss him a lot."

"The good Nick?"

Tess bit her lip. "Nick . . . changes," she said finally. "Back and forth. Deep inside, I think there's a real Nick, but there's mostly this plastic Nick who's climbing to the top of his profession and doesn't care about anything else. And I hate the way he acts when he's like that."

"Like forgetting you exist?"

"Like that, yes, but also—" Tess started to walk again and Gina tagged along beside her "—the way he is with Welch. Respectful all the time so he'll get the contract. Or the way he goes to the opera because it gets his picture on the society page. And the thing is, for a while I thought it was just a stage he was passing through. That once he'd made it, he'd go back to being himself." She looked at Gina. "Now, I'm not sure he knows which one is real—the nice guy or the climber. And I love the one and I hate the other and I'm afraid, I'm really afraid that I'll end up with the other one. Jekyll."

"Instead of Heckle?" Gina shook her head. "I could never tell them apart."

"No, instead of Hyde."

"I thought Hyde was the monster."

"Take a close look at Jekyll sometime," Tess said. "Especially if there's money and a promotion involved."

"Maybe you should give him another chance," Gina said. "I mean, he's really interested in you—" she stopped as Tess gave her a look of contempt "—well, at least part of the time, and last night must have been pretty spectacular or you wouldn't care what he was, and you like his car, too." Gina shrugged. "I'd go for it."

Tess looked at her in disbelief. "Life is more than great sex and a nice car."

"Well, yeah. But not a lot more."

Tess glared at Gina in startled indignation, only to find her grinning at her. It was the first smile she'd seen on Gina since they'd come to Kentucky, so she smiled back, relieved that Gina was showing signs of recovering.

"You know," Tess said, putting her arm around Gina, "you're a nice woman, DaCosta. But we have to work on your depth. You have none."

"I'm practicing to be a yuppie." Gina's grin faded. "Not that I'll ever be one."

Tess frowned. "Listen, I meant it when I told you that the thing at dinner did not matter, but I've also got to tell you that lusting after Park Patterson is a bad idea."

"I know," Gina said. "Don't worry about me. You got enough trouble of your own to handle."

"This is true," Tess said, and they both turned back to the house, sunk in gloom.

LUNCH WAS NOT GOOD.

The food, of course, was impeccable, since Henderson had been in charge of that part. But not even Henderson could have saved the conversation between Nick and Tess.

"Just tell me what I did wrong," Nick said under his breath, trying to look unconcerned so no one would catch on they were fighting.

"I don't want to talk about it," Tess said.

"If you don't talk about it, I'll probably do it again. Although I'm damned if I see what's so bad about making love to you all night."

"It wasn't the night. It was the morning," Tess said.

"We didn't make love this morning."

"Right," Tess said. "Pass the salt."

"If you want to make love, just *say* so. I'm not a mind reader."

"I didn't want to make love. Well, actually I did, but that's not it."

"Well, then *what?*"

"Troubles, Jamieson?" Welch called from the other end of the table.

"Not at all," Nick called back, smiling. "Just enjoying another great meal, sir."

"You are disgusting," Tess said to Nick.

"What did I do?" Nick asked, but she turned away from him to talk to the man next to her.

TESS MANAGED to keep the chill on through lunch and up to the reading, but then her curiosity got the better of her. In the living room, Henderson had set up rows of carved walnut chairs, their seats covered in navy-and-brown tapestry, so that the place looked like a lecture hall done by *Architectural Digest*. The chairs were filling up with people who had clout and prestige and really good tailors, leaving Tess to puzzle over why Welch had chosen these guests. They were so upscale, so obviously unlike him, yet he was gruffly pleased to see them there. The only thing she could come up with was that he was courting them so that they'd push his book, an unlikely motive for a literary icon.

"Does Welch need these people?" Tess asked Nick, forgetting that she was mad at him.

"Honey, everybody needs these people," Nick said. "There are two senators and a governor here."

Tess frowned. "I know that. What does that have to do with literature?"

"Nothing." Nick frowned in thought, and Tess knew he was moving into analytical gear. "I think it's about public relations. I think Welch wants to move beyond writing. I've been watching him all weekend, and I think he's going after a political career. He was talking to Tricia Sigler about Decker at lunch today, and that's a high-profile place, a lot of powerful parents send their kids there, and he's been very tight with Bob O'Donnell all weekend—"

"Bob O'Donnell?"

"Republican party honcho here in Kentucky," Nick said. "I think Welch sees himself as a right-wing standard-bearer. And you know, it's not a dumb idea. It's not a bad time for a neoconservative to make a move. There's some backlash building up against the Democratic administration. And he's still fairly young. Plenty of time to start a political career. A Senate seat would be a good move for him." Nick relaxed back into his chair. "Which also takes care of the other mystery, now that I come to think of it. Park told me that Welch doesn't like his father, Kent Patterson, and never has, so why is he wining and dining us?"

"Why?" Tess asked, totally confused.

"Because Kent has clout in the social circles that Welch needs if he wants to get elected," Nick said promptly. "Kent knows people with money who would like Welch's politics. Kent may be a lousy lawyer, but he knows how to network. So Welch invited Park and me down here to see if we have the brains to do some minimal law work for him. Then he can give us a contract to make the connection with Kent." Nick shook his head in admiration. "You know, I'm starting to like Welch a lot better."

"I'm starting to like him a lot less," Tess said. "All this sucking up. What happened to the good old days when rich white men just bought their way into office?"

"Inflation," Nick said. "Nobody's that rich anymore." He smiled at Tess. "You know, I owe you for this weekend. Welch really likes you, and that's made points for me." He patted Tess on the shoulder, and she made a disgusted face at him. "No, I really mean it. I watched the two of you at lunch. He likes the hard time you give him as much as you like giving it to him. I'd be jealous except I know you're crazy about me."

"That was last night, this is today," Tess said, but he grinned at her confidently. She looked away just in time to see Welch come into the room for the reading.

He was imposing as he took his stand behind the massive walnut podium that Henderson had placed at one end of the room, and when he began to speak in general on the ravages that liberalism and feminism had wrought on the country, it was obvious that he was speaking to a mostly receptive audience. It was also obvious that Nick, as usual, was right on the money. Welch was prepping for a move into politics.

"I don't like this," Gina whispered to her.

"I know," Tess whispered back. "I know."

"If you listen to those people," Welch was saying, "you'd think life was just a fairy tale where everybody is good and honest and things turn out happily ever after. But you know, I always had my doubts about those happily-ever-afters. Anne Sexton isn't the only one who wondered about what happened when the chickens came home to roost." He chuckled and then caught Tess's eye. She stuck out her tongue at him, and he chuckled again, but this time there seemed to be a nervous edge to his laugh.

"So my book is about what happens *after* the happily-ever-after," Welch said. "Which is why it's called *After the Ever After*. The prologue is a fairy tale about a young woman who comes of age in the sixties. Her name is Cinderellen—" the audience tittered politely "—and she buys into happily-ever-after in a big way. This is the end of the tale."

Then Welch began to read a scene in which his heroine stood up at the ball and made a speech defending the importance of the environment over big business, a speech that instantly won the heart of the prince, and Tess's heart stopped. It wasn't just the snide tone Welch used—a tone that made people in the audience first smile in sardonic amusement and then laugh in outright derision—it was the words, words that were so familiar to her that she recited them silently in unison with Welch as he read, finishing with: "And from then on

Cinderellen and the prince looked for the good in every day and tried to make sure they had a part in creating some of it."

That got a big laugh, and Tess felt the room swoop around her as her whole body went hot with anger. He was telling the CinderTess story, Lanny's story, and he was making people laugh at it. It was her story, and he was degrading it, degrading her and everything she believed in. She was so rigid with suppressed rage that Nick turned to see what was wrong.

"Tess?" he whispered.

She shook her head, trying to marshal her thoughts.

Welch then segued into Cinderellen's story thirty years later. She was swamped with debts, dragged down by the poor people she was trying to help, unable to keep her small family business going because of environmental restrictions and saddled with a prince who had turned out to be a vapid do-gooding fool. As the audience nodded, enjoying the expected disasters that had befallen the naive heroine, Tess reminded herself to take deep breaths, to concentrate, to do anything to control the rising anger that swamped her because of what Welch was doing to her story.

To Lanny's story.

"I'm going to kill him," she whispered under her breath, which prompted Nick to shush her.

Welch finished the scene with Cinderellen's emancipation speech: she was mad as hell and not going to take it anymore. Then Welch stopped reading to sketch in Cinderellen's transformation. She streamlined her company by laying off workers and saved a bundle by not helping the poor, but that wasn't enough. She went to the best plastic surgeon in the land and had him transform her back into the beauty she'd been at the ball. Then she set out to tell her story again. Only this time, she was going to do it right, using all her feminine wiles. The last scene he read was a comic seduction scene in which Cinderellen used her newly recovered beauty to seduce the head of the Environmental Protection Agency into exempting her company from environmental controls, manipulating him with a speech on the importance of business over the environment as she slithered over first his desk and then his body. As a piece of satire it was dead-on, a perfect parody of Cinderellen's original speech. People were falling off their chairs laughing.

Tess was catatonic with rage.

"What's wrong?" Nick leaned closer as people applauded at the end of the reading. "Are you all right?"

"No." Tess turned to him. "We have to stop him. He can't publish this book."

"Tess," Nick said warningly. "You are not going to interfere. It's his book."

"No, it's not. He plagiarized."

Nick closed his eyes. "No. Don't tell me this."

Tess shook her head. "He plagiarized. I know that story. It's not his."

"ALL RIGHT." Nick shut the door to Welch's study behind Tess and Park and Gina. "Explain this to me."

Tess cast one blindly incurious look around the room, registering expensive paneling, Oriental carpets, a huge leather-and-brass sofa and soulless sets of leather-bound books on walnut bookcases with glass fronts. *Money,* she thought. *It always comes back to money.*

"Tess?" Nick prompted.

"He plagiarized," she replied. "That prologue about Cinderellen? He stole it. Word for word, the whole thing. He stole it."

"Why would anybody plagiarize that garbage?" Nick asked. "It was god-awful. The good stuff came later. I just hope the critics make it through the early garbage to get to the good stuff."

"You're not listening to me," Tess said. "It's never going to get to the critics. He plagiarized, and I'm going to stop him."

"*No!*" Nick and Park said simultaneously, and Gina said softly, "Oh, no." Then Nick pushed Tess down into the padded leather desk chair and sat down on the desk in front of her.

"That would not be a good idea," he said.

"Why not?" Tess demanded.

Park snorted. "Because there's a lot of money at stake here, that's why not."

Nick held up his hand. "Will you let me handle this?" he said to Park. "Please?" He turned back to Tess. "It's like this. We're guests in this man's house, and now you want to accuse him of plagiarism. I know you'll find this hard to understand, but it doesn't seem appropriate under the circumstances."

"The hell with appropriate," Tess said. "This is a moral issue. No, it's more than a moral issue. It's my life he's trashing. It's everything Lanny ever gave me, and I'm going to confront him."

"Confront me with it first," Nick said.

"Do not let her talk you into this," Park warned.

Tess appealed to Park. "Doesn't the fact that he stole part of that book make any difference to you? You're a lawyer. You're supposed to uphold the law."

"That's the police," Park said. "Don't get us confused. We make a lot more money. And we're going to keep on making a lot more money if you keep your mouth shut about plagiarism."

"I don't believe this," Tess said. "You want him to get away with it."

"Wait a minute," Nick said. "We don't even know what he's getting away with. Explain."

"Oh, great," Park said.

Tess shot him a dirty look, then concentrated on Nick. "When I was about eight, we lived on a commune near Yellow Springs. Here in Ohio."

"I know where Yellow Springs is," Nick said. "Go on."

"Bunch of hippies," Park put in.

"It was a nice commune," Tess flared. "Anyway, one day not too long after we got there, this guy showed up." She bit her lip, the hollow feeling in the pit of her stomach growing as she remembered how special Lanny had been and how Welch had just raped his story. "He was really wonderful," she said. "He was probably in his early twenties. A big husky guy." She smiled. "I thought he was a mountain. Big and broad with long brown hair and a big brown beard. Big ears. Everything about him was bigger than life."

"Great," Nick said. "Get to the point."

"His name was Lanny."

"Is this important?" Park asked. "Because Gina and I are missing cocktails."

"Shut up, Park," Nick said. "Get to the point, Tess."

"He told me that same story," she said. "The prologue story. Word for word, it's Lanny's story."

"And you remember it thirty years later?" Nick asked. "Come on."

"He told it to me over and over again the whole summer," Tess said. "Every time he told it, he added something, another task the heroine had to do, another problem she had to solve, and it got to be really long. When he left at the end of the summer, he wrote it all down for me, and Elise used to read parts of it to me every night for the two years we lived there. I know big chunks of it by heart." She glared up at Nick. "And your great American author was reading that same story. I could recite parts of it with him. He stole that story."

"Who's Elise?" Nick asked, confused.

"My mother."

"And she read you a story about this Ellen?" Park said. "I don't believe it."

"No. My story was about CinderTess."

Park rolled his eyes.

"Lanny wrote that story for me," Tess said to Nick, ignoring Park. "And Welch stole it, and I'm going to—"

"Are you sure, Tess?" Nick said. "This is serious."

"I *told* you," Tess said. "He wrote it for *me*. It was my story. And at the end Lanny always said, 'And CinderTess and the prince always looked for the best in every day and made sure they had a part in creating some of it.'" She stared up at Nick defiantly. "And that's exactly how Welch ended that part he read to us."

"Could be the same," Nick said reluctantly. "So you're saying that Welch is using parts of the same story."

"No," Tess said. "He's using *all* of the same story. Word for word. And even worse, he's making fun of it. He's making *my* story sound stupid and..." She caught her breath and tried to slow herself down. "Look, the CinderTess story was important to me. In fact, sometimes I think it had more impact on me than my parents did. I know Lanny did." She stopped and looked at Nick, her jaw tight with determination. "I know it sounds childish to you, but basically Lanny taught me how to live my life with that story, and I'm not going to let some aging neoconservative with writer's block turn it into an antifeminist tirade. I'm going to talk to Welch."

"Wait a minute." Nick folded his arms and stared down at her with disgust. "Let me get this straight. The reason you're always rushing in to save the world is that this guy told you a fairy tale?"

"Didn't you have any book when you were a kid that affected you like that?" Tess asked. "You know, like *The Velveteen Rabbit*? Love is what makes you real?"

"People should be more careful about what they read to their kids," Park said. "Some of this stuff sounds dangerous."

"Well, kids just don't get caught up in the *Wall Street Journal*, Park," Tess snapped. "They tend to be deeper than adults." She turned back to Nick. "But the important thing is that he's taken the story and turned it inside out. It's as if he'd rewritten *The Little Engine That Could* so that it *couldn't*."

"I had that book," Park said.

"I did, too," Gina said.

Park smiled down at Gina. "That was a good one, wasn't it?"

"Exactly!" Tess said before Gina could mention any other childhood favorites. She glared at Park. "Wouldn't you be angry if somebody stole that book and made the train fail?"

Park looked startled. "Well, yes. But that's not—"

"Well, that's why I'm angry," Tess said. "He didn't just steal Lanny's story, he made it sound . . . stupid. Foolish."

"It was stupid," Nick said.

"No, it wasn't. Not if you were a little kid. It still isn't if you have any values at all."

"Oh, hell, don't start," Nick said. "Let me think about this."

Park sat down beside him on the edge of the desk. "Don't bother." He turned to Tess. "This was a handwritten manuscript, right? Not published in any way?"

"Right. But that doesn't—"

"And this was in the sixties?" Park said.

Tess counted back. "About sixty-five or sixty-six. I can find out for sure."

"Then legally it doesn't matter," Park said. "According to the copyright law of 1976, any work automatically comes under copyright as soon as it's written. But before that, which means the sixties, we're dealing with the 1947 law that says works not produced for sale must be registered with the copyright office, and I don't imagine your hippie buddy did that. Of course, since he wrote it down and gave a copy to your mother, that could be construed as publication, but not enough to remove it from fair assumption that it was public domain. I think Welch is covered."

Tess listened to him openmouthed and then turned to Nick. "This is Park? This walking textbook of loopholes is Park?"

Nick shrugged. "I told you—nobody knows contract law like Park."

Park went on as if he hadn't heard them. "Plus, part of the 1976 law says that plagiarism is only an issue when the new work affects the potential market of the work in question. Frankly, from what I heard, there is no potential market for that drivel. In fact, if Welch's book makes it big, your hippie buddy could actually profit because then there might be a market for his stuff. Besides, Welch can't copyright something that belongs to someone else even if he uses it in a copyrighted book. So your buddy could still claim copyright to his old story and publish it." Park stopped, struck by a thought. "I wonder if he's represented by anybody. What did you say his name was?"

"I don't care what the law says," Tess said, recovering from her shock at Park's sudden acuity. "I know Welch stole it and that's wrong. It belongs to Lanny. The least he could do is give Lanny credit. Lanny was wonderful." She stood up. "And I'm going to tell Welch—"

"No!" both men said again.

"Just wait," Nick said. "Wait until Park and I can look into it."

Park scowled. "Why? I just told you, legally there's no prob—"

"Well, there may be a problem morally," Nick said. "Especially if a thousand enraged former hippies start writing op-ed pieces and faxing them from their Mercedes."

"Oh, come on," Park said. "All from one little Ohio commune?"

"He moved on," Nick reminded him. "He stayed for a while and then moved on." He turned to Tess. "How long was he with the commune?"

Tess shrugged, still simmering with anger. "Just for the summer. But then, who cares about Lanny? Let's protect the great Norbert Welch and all of his millions first."

"Tess, concentrate," Nick persisted. "About Lanny. Did other people hear the stories?"

"Of course," Tess said. "There were a lot of us kids there. CinderTess was one of our bedtime stories that summer."

Nick frowned. "Where did he go when he left? Did he move on to another commune?"

"I don't know. I don't even know where *we* went next. Pennsylvania, probably."

"So he could have told this story across the country," Nick said. "Thousands could have heard it."

Tess smiled, triumphant at this new turn of events. "Yup. Just think of them all out there, waiting to pounce when this thing hits the bookstores." She looked at the two men virtuously. "We have to confront Norbert Welch. For his own good."

"No," they said again, but the vehemence was gone from their voices, and Nick looked thoughtful. Park just looked annoyed.

"Can we sleep on this?" Park said finally. "Welch isn't publishing this damn thing tomorrow. Can we just wait awhile and give this some consideration first?"

"And then we'll confront him?" Tess demanded.

"Maybe," Nick said. "Listen, we don't want to rush into anything here. There's a lot riding on this. My partnership, for one thing. If that book doesn't get published, I'm out in the cold."

Tess looked at him in disgust. "I can't believe what a Yuppie scum you are. I should have known you weren't a prince."

Park looked at him in equal disgust. "You had to bring her, didn't you? It had to be Tess." He shook his head and walked out of the room.

Gina looked after him miserably, turned and looked at Tess in equal misery, and then followed Park.

Nick sighed. "It's not going to do us any good to go rushing around shouting 'Plagiarism' at a crowded book reading. Give it a rest and let me think about it."

"Until Monday," Tess said. "I'll give you until Monday. Then I'm talking to Norbert Welch, and if he won't see reason, I'm going to the press."

"You are one hell of a fun date," Nick said.

"Well, I wouldn't worry about it, since I'm never going anywhere with you again." With that Tess stomped out of the room.

"Give me that in writing," Nick called to her retreating back. Then he leaned back in his chair and groaned.

TESS CONTENTED HERSELF with being barely civil to Welch when she said her goodbyes as the afternoon ended. Nick, of course, was more than civil, even though Welch genially told him he needed more time to consider the contract.

"I'll call you next week, Jamieson," he said, shaking hands with him and entirely ignoring a confused Park. "Maybe we can have dinner. Bring Tess. I like her."

"We'd enjoy that, sir," Nick said, wondering how he was going to talk Tess into a long business dinner when she had just vowed never to see him again.

Tess meanwhile was saying goodbye to the only man in the area she was still speaking to. "I really enjoyed watching you this weekend, Henderson," she said, and then she stood on her toes and kissed the old man on the cheek. "You're a wonder."

"Thank you, Miss Newhart," Henderson said impassively.

When they were in the car, Nick grinned at her. "You're going to give that man ideas."

"At least he doesn't steal them like his boss," Tess said, and Nick gave up. She was hopeless. Sleeping with her had been great, well, more than great, and he did care about her, but she was going to be death on his career no matter what he did. As much as he wanted her, as much as he liked being with her, he was going to have to stop calling her.

Which was just as well, since she'd told him she was never going to speak to him again. The last time she'd told him that, it had taken him over a month to get her to talk to him. He didn't have that kind of time to waste on any woman, let alone one who was a career assassin.

After an hour passed without Tess saying anything, Nick stole a glance at her. She was frowning into the distance.

"What's wrong now?" he said.

"I need to do something about Lanny." Tess sounded distracted. "I need to help Gina, too. You were right—she's leaving the road and trying to get a job at the Charles Theater. I don't know anyone there, so that's a problem. But first I need to go home and make some phone calls. I need to try to find Lanny or at least the manuscript, or nobody is ever going to listen to me about this." She looked over at Nick and all the anger was gone from her eyes. "I know you hate this because of the partnership. I understand. I even understand that you can't do anything about this just on my word alone. I'm not telling you that I'm going to find that manuscript just to make you mad. I'm not even mad myself anymore. But I want you to know I'm going to find that manuscript. I have to. It's really important to me."

"Why is it so important?" Nick asked. "What is this guy to you?" He tried to keep the jealousy out of his voice because it was ridiculous to be jealous of a guy that Tess had known when she was a kid, especially since he was never going to see her again.

"Because I loved him," Tess said, and Nick felt his jealousy flare in spite of his good intentions.

"You were six—"

Tess interrupted him. "I was eight," she said. "Not that it matters. At first I just adored him the way kids do movie stars. He was so big and so full of life and so . . . full of ideas and *stories*. Wonderful stories. And then after a while, he was a lot more. Like a big brother and a father and a mother and a best friend. He paid *attention* to me. And he listened to what I had to say, like it was important. He'd ask me questions and listen to the answers. And he made more sense than anybody else around me. He was always really gruff and acted like he was exasperated to be spending time on me, but he wasn't, and he taught me *useful* things. I mean, Daniel would tell me it was important to live a peaceful life in harmony with all things."

"Daniel?"

"My father," Tess said. "But the thing was, the gang of kids at the commune could be pretty nasty, and it's hard to live a peaceful life when you've got little Nazis pushing you around. And it wasn't so much that I was afraid to fight back but that I didn't know how. So I asked Lanny about it, and he said the key to fighting was never to fight unless the cause was so great that you couldn't bear not to defend it and the losses you were going to suffer were things you could afford to lose. And then he said, if I did decide to fight, the thing to remember was that

I was going to get hurt, because that was what happened in a fight, so I might as well get myself reconciled to it in the beginning and then it wouldn't matter when it happened."

"Great advice for a kid," Nick said, trying not to sound as grumpy as he felt.

"It was great advice for anybody," Tess said. "I actually ended up walking away from most fights because I didn't care that much about what they were hassling me about. And when I did fight back, I went in no-holds-barred because I knew I was going to get beat up, anyway. After a couple of times, the other kids pretty much left me alone. That was always the way it was with Lanny. He told you good stuff, true stuff that worked. Like the CinderTess story. No matter how many changes he made in it, it always ended with the real happily-ever-after coming from trying to make the world a better place. And that's what Welch made fun of. He made fun of Lanny. And when he did that, he made fun of everything I believe in." Tess turned to face Nick again. "I have to fight this one. And I know I'm going to get hurt. I know Welch is tougher than I am and richer than I am and more powerful than I am. And I know you're going to help him, not me. But I can't walk away from Lanny. I can't walk away from everything I believe in."

Nick was silent for a while. "Look," he said finally. "If it's that important to you, I'll help."

Tess blinked at him. "What about the contract?"

Nick shrugged. "I need to know everything I can about this damn book if I get the contract. And if he really has plagiarized, I need to know." Nick stopped for a moment, trying to imagine the horror that a real plagiarism suit could turn out to be. Maybe he should be grateful to Tess for discovering this early, while he could handle it. "So here's the deal. I'll help you when you need help, and I'll stay out of your way the rest of the time so you can do this your way. Okay?"

She didn't say anything, and he stole a look at her. "Tess?"

"It's more than okay," she said. "I keep forgetting you can be like this. I get so upset over the press-for-success part of you that I forget about this part."

"That's me, a man of many parts," Nick said.

"Thank you," Tess said. "Thank you very much."

"Sure," Nick said. "Think of it as a goodbye gift."

They finished the drive deep in their own thoughts, and Nick had almost reconciled himself to never being with her again. It was the only logical plan. In fact, it was so obviously logical, he wasn't sure why he was trying to find a hole in it.

By the time they were on the third flight of stairs to her apartment, he was convinced he was doing the right thing. Just drop off her stuff and escape. Just walk right on out.

"Listen, I can't stay. . ." he began, as they neared the top of the flight to her floor.

"You certainly can't," Tess said as she reached the landing. "I'm grateful to you for offering to help, but we're never going to—"

He bumped into her from behind when she froze at the top of the stairs. Then he peered around her.

Her apartment door had been kicked in.

7

"OH, NO," TESS SAID, and went to look through the remains of the door.

Nick grabbed her arm to stop her. "Let me go first."

The neighbor across the hall opened his door, clutching his beer can with one hand and scratching the strip of belly his T-shirt couldn't stretch to cover with his other. "Your apartment got hit," he said to Tess with a total lack of interest. "Last night. I called the police. You're supposed to call 'em."

"Thank you very much." Nick pushed past Tess to stand in the doorway. "That's very helpful."

Tess said, "Thank you, Stanley," a little dazedly, and then followed Nick to peer in behind him.

The place had been tossed and trashed. Drawers were upended, furniture overturned, and all the furniture cushions were slashed and bleeding stuffing on the floor.

"Oh, no," Tess said again, her voice little more than a sigh.

"You have any enemies?" Nick asked.

Tess shook her head. "It's not personal. This has happened before to other people in the building. It's not me."

"It's happened before and you didn't tell me?"

"We weren't speaking," Tess flared. "And I was handling it. I reported the landlord."

Nick surveyed the ruined door. "Oh, yeah, you were handling it." He shook his head. "Well, from now on, I'm handling it."

"Excuse me, I don't think so—" Tess began.

"They did the same thing to the apartment one floor down last week," Stanley volunteered. "Just kids looking for cash."

"Just kids," Nick said. "Little rascals." He turned to Tess. "Pack up anything you want to keep. You're coming home with me. No arguments."

Tess set her jaw, prepared to fight. "I thought you couldn't wait to get rid of me."

"Well, yes, but I meant out of *my* life, not out of life in general," Nick said, ignoring her to peer through the door. "You are not staying here. If you'd rather stay with Gina, fine, but you're not staying here."

"Gina has one room, an efficiency," Tess said. "She couldn't squeeze Angela in, let alone me." She stopped suddenly.

"Fine," Nick said, oblivious to her silence. "Then you're staying at my place. There's a guest bedroom. Your virtue is safe." He turned and saw her face, white with fear. "What's wrong?"

"Angela," Tess said, and bit her lip. "I don't see Angela."

Nick moved to put his arms around her, and she leaned against him gratefully. "Angela is not a stupid cat," he said into her hair. "When the Brady Bunch showed up, she probably went out the window." He tightened his arms around her and then said, "Come on. Let's get your stuff and go."

Tess nodded, and Nick moved cautiously ahead of her into the apartment. He checked her bedroom before she could, to make sure Angela wasn't bleeding into the bedspread. Not only was there no Angela, there was no bedspread. The bedroom was as ransacked as the rest of the apartment. He turned back to Tess. "Pack."

She opened her mouth to argue, and he overrode her. "Look, you want to find a new place tomorrow, no problem. But you can't stay here. Not ever again. I'd never sleep again waiting for these guys to come back and do to you what they did to the couch."

"Okay," Tess said. "All right."

Nick watched her rescue what she could from the place, brushing off her mismatched sofa pillows and picking up odds and ends of God knew what. And while he watched, he tried a little deep breathing to calm the fear and rage that were making him insane. If he hadn't dragged her off to Kentucky, she could have been here, in this dump. Pure luck of the draw. The thought of losing her in any way made him cold, but losing her like this would have been—

"I'm all right," Tess said, and he looked up to see her standing in the doorway with a laundry basket full of clothes. "I know you're upset, but I'm all right and I'm leaving with you and I'm not coming back. I promise."

"Thank you," Nick said. "Is there anything you want in the kitchen?"

"Yes," Tess said. "But I don't suppose it's in one piece anymore. Did you look in there?"

"It's not good," Nick said. "Come on. I'll help."

They managed to rescue a few odd pieces of china and glassware.

"Was this stuff your mother's?" Nick asked, and Tess looked at him oddly.

"Elise doesn't have stuff," she said. "This is just stuff I found in thrift stores that I liked." She gazed at it sadly. "Maybe I liked it because it's the kind of stuff that mothers are supposed to give to their daughters. That's pathetic." She stood up, leaving the china on the floor. "I really don't want it. All I really want is Angela."

"I'll work on it," Nick said. "Get your things together, and I'll take the first load down to the car."

He took the laundry basket out on the landing and knocked on the door across the hall. The neighbor looked out. "Yeah?"

"You know that big black cat that belongs to Tess?" Nick said.

"Yeah?"

"I'll give you a hundred bucks if I can pick up that cat to-morrow."

"How the hell am I supposed to get that cat back?" Stanley whined.

"Well, if I were you, I'd buy about ten cans of cat food and sit over there until the cat comes back," Nick said.

"That could be hours."

"That's what I'm paying for," Nick said, handing over his business card. "Take it or leave it."

Tess came to the door carrying her duffel bag and Nick's suitcase. "This is everything."

"Great," Nick said. "Let's go."

TESS SAT LOST in thought on the way to Nick's, grateful for the silence he gave her, trying to figure out why she felt so torn. It wasn't that she loved her apartment; she hated it. Nothing ever worked right, and the street was noisy, full of shouting and squealing brakes, and even now and then a gunshot. But it had been hers, and now she was going to Nick's, and she was pretty sure that wherever Nick's was, there wouldn't be screams or shots or cockroaches or broken anything. She was pretty sure it would be clean and safe and expensive and tempting as hell.

Then Nick turned off the road into his driveway, and it was worse than she suspected.

The house wasn't large, but it was beautiful, an architect's miniature masterpiece of white planes and angles bisected by gleaming glass that reflected the moonlight. She'd been prepared to resist clapboard colonial or petite plantation or even pseudo-cedar Frank Lloyd Wright, but this was such a work of art that only a person blinded by prejudice could find it anything but lovely.

"Do you like it?" Nick asked when he'd cut the engine.

"I've never seen anything so beautiful," Tess said, and she felt him relax next to her. "When you brought me out here before it was finished, I never dreamed it would look like this. Who designed it? You?"

"Not exactly." Nick eased down in his seat a little, surveying the house. "When I was in law school, a buddy of mine got in trouble. I helped him out, did all the legal legwork and saved his butt. He was a senior in architecture, and he took me out for a beer, and after a few, we started talking about the perfect house, and a month later he gave me the plans for this. So I saved up and bought the land, then I saved some more and built the house. It took me a while."

Tess watched his face as he looked at his house, seeing the pride and love there.

"The builders were the best," he said, "and the irony is, my buddy's a big name now. Preston Delaney. People come by and photograph it because it's an early, pure Delaney. I've only been in it a couple of weeks, and somebody's already offered me twice what it cost to build it."

Tess rolled her eyes. "Another investment."

Nick shook his head. "Nope, it's more than that. Wait until you see inside. It's perfect. It was done a month after you left." His grin faded. "That was one of the biggest disappointments about your dumping me. You never got to see it." He turned to her in the moonlight. "I know we're finished with each other, but I'm glad you're here to see it."

Tess bit her lip. "Thank you for inviting me to stay. I'll try not to get it dirty."

Nick patted her knee and then got out to open the car door for her while she stared at the house with fear and longing.

The interior left her speechless. The ground floor was one big room bisected by black lacquered folding doors with a staircase winding up the middle of it. To her right, through partially opened doors, Tess could see a massive ebony Parsons dining table and black lacquered chairs. To the left, huge overstuffed couches faced each other across thick rya rugs, flanking a cavernous white brick fireplace on one wall and a built-in wide-screen TV on another. The back wall was all glass looking out on an oval pool that reflected the moonlight like marcasite.

Except for the dining-room furniture, every single thing in the place was white. Tess felt very small and very dingy. She moved to one of the couches, touching it and then jerking her hand away.

"What's the matter?" Nick asked.

"This couch is suede," Tess said.

"I know."

"Real suede?" Tess asked, knowing it was a dumb question. If it was Nick's, it was real.

"Of course it's real suede."

"You have white suede couches," Tess said and closed her eyes. "Do you live here? Does anybody live here?"

"Don't you like it?"

"It's incredible. But I am definitely going to get it dirty."

"That's why a cleaning woman comes in twice a week," Nick said.

"Well, that's a relief." Tess turned to the stairs. "Bedroom up here?"

"Three," Nick said. "Take your pick."

"Which one are you in?"

"The one at the back. Big bed. Black satin spread. The guest room is at the front."

"Black," Tess said. "You know, I don't mean to criticize, but this place could use some color."

"I like it this way. It looks expensive." Nick started up the stairs with the duffel and the suitcase. "Where do you want this stuff?"

"Guest room." Tess said, and followed him with the laundry basket.

TESS LAY AWAKE that night, listening for the screams and the shouts that weren't there, trying not to worry about Angela and feeling guilty because she was so safe. The other tenants didn't have rich, depraved conservative lawyers to sweep them off into sinful luxury. And then there was Gina, looking at Park with puppy-dog eyes. And the Foundation kids, now that she'd shot herself in the foot with the Sigler woman. And Lanny. The other problems were more pressing, but Lanny was the one she owed the most. Lanny had been there for her when she was eight; now she was going to be there for him.

She tossed and turned for another hour, shuffling her worries like a deck of cards. When she finally couldn't stand it any longer, she slipped out of bed and tiptoed down the stairs, careful not to wake Nick, and went out to the pool. She stripped off her T-shirt and underpants, dove into the water and began to swim laps to exorcise her demons.

One lap for the apartment-house tenants and their unlocked doors.

One lap for Gina and her doomed love life and her job search.

One lap for the kids at the Foundation and their imperiled futures.

One lap for Lanny and his trashed vision.

One lap for Nick and his infuriating double personality.

Only one lap didn't do it. Once she started to think about Nick warm in that damn black bed upstairs, she swam faster, but it didn't help. All the images of him she'd ever tortured herself with came back—Nick laughing at her at the touch football game that had started it all, Nick's arms in that rag of a sweatshirt as he teased her about her laundry, Nick beautiful in evening clothes—but now she had new memories, memories of Nick hot and naked, his body moving over hers, and she got dizzy just thinking about it, so dizzy that at the end of the last lap, she clung to the edge of the pool and gasped for breath.

"You okay?" she heard Nick say, and she looked up to see him standing there, in black silk boxers, his hair still tousled from his pillow.

He looked wonderful.

Tess groaned and let herself slip under the water.

She felt Nick's hand grab her arm and drag her ruthlessly to the surface.

"I know you're depressed, dummy," Nick said, holding on to her. "But don't drown yourself in my pool. My insurance rates will go up. Not to mention I'll never get another date again if it gets out that being with me makes women suicidal."

"I'm not suicidal," Tess said, and then realized he was never going to make love to her again. "Well, maybe I am."

"Actually what you are is naked." Nick sounded distracted, but he didn't let go of her arm.

"It's a private pool." Tess was too depressed to argue with any enthusiasm. "It's not illegal."

"No, but it's probably immoral," Nick said. "Whatever it is, I like it. Let's go back to my bed and discuss it."

Tess blinked up at him, treading water a little faster. "I thought we were finished."

"Well, we were until your apartment got trashed and I thought about losing you, and then you ended up naked in my pool," Nick said. "I remember being sure I never wanted to see you again. I just don't remember why at the moment."

Tess sighed. "It was probably something about your career. Everything with you is."

"What career?"

"Really?" Tess said, her voice suddenly bright with hope.

"I'm thinking about becoming a pool boy," Nick said. "You meet such naked people."

Tess jerked the arm he was holding and yanked him into the pool.

"Hey," he sputtered when he surfaced, but by then she'd wrapped herself around him and found his mouth with hers, and they slipped under the water as she kissed him.

Nick kicked them both to the surface again and held her tight against him as he tried to get his breath back. Tess trailed kisses down his neck, licking the water from his skin with her tongue, loving the feel of the muscle against her mouth.

"A bed," Nick gasped. "I have this great bed—"

"Here," Tess said, and kissed him. She felt him relax into her as he pulled her hips tight against his, and she wrapped her legs around him again, feeling the slick wet silk of his shorts against her thighs. "Those have got to go," she told him, and began to slide her fingers under the waistband to yank them down.

"Wait a minute," Nick said, grabbing her hand, still trying to keep them afloat. "About my bed—"

"Here," Tess said, tugging downward on his shorts.

"The neighbors—" Nick said, tugging upward.

"Here," Tess said tugging harder.

"I really think my bed—" Nick tried again, prying her fingers from his waistband.

Tess gave a scream of fury and pushed him away. "Forget it," she said. "Just forget it."

"Look, is this the romantic thing again?" Nick groped through the water for her again. "Because I don't see what's so romantic about a damn pool."

"It's not just romantic," Tess said, kicking backward to get away from him. "It's spontaneous. It's sexy. It doesn't feel like a damn career move!" She was so mad she dove underwater to get away from him, and when she surfaced he was gone.

Well, good. The hell with him. If she'd given in, she'd have ended up having sex in bedrooms for the rest of her life. Which of course, wouldn't have been an entirely bad thing since it would have been with Nick. Which was actually pretty cosmic when she thought about it. But she wasn't going to think about it because he was the most unspontaneous, conservative, let's-plan-every-move man she'd ever met. Which did, of course, often lead to great sex since he made sure . . .

Oh, hell.

Tess dove for the bottom of the pool again and swam across it, only to swallow half the pool when somebody grabbed her ankle.

Nick hauled her to the surface, patting her on the back while she choked.

"Don't *do* that!" she said when she could talk. "I almost drowned."

"Don't exaggerate," Nick said, and kissed her.

"I thought you left," she said when she came up for air. "Is this come-up-to-my-bed, part two, because if so . . ." She stopped, distracted by the realization that he wasn't wearing his shorts.

"No," Nick said, pulling her against him. "This is the-hell-with-the-neighbors-but-I-had-to-get-a-condom, part one. Do you know if chlorine has any effect on latex?"

"No idea." Tess locked her legs around him, not caring what chlorine did to latex.

"Well, let's find out," Nick said, and then they almost did drown.

WHEN TESS WOKE UP the next morning, there was a note on the black silk pillow beside her with a twenty-dollar bill and a key.

She looked at the ceiling in exasperation and then picked up the note. "Dear Tess," it read. "The twenty bucks is for cab fare so you can get out of the house today, so stop scowling at the ceiling. I took some swimming-pool water with me to the office so I can snort the chlorine and think of you all day. I'll bring dinner with me when I get home at six. I'm glad your apartment got trashed. Love, Nick."

She cocked an eyebrow at the note and smiled. It wasn't "How do I love thee, let me count the ways," but it wasn't bad at all.

She snuggled back down under the comforter and thought about her day ahead. She had to go to the police station to fill out forms on the break-in. She had to call Alan Sigler to tell him that she definitely wanted the job at Decker even if his wife did hate her. She had to stop by the Foundation and catch up on her tutoring. She had to call her mother and ask about Lanny. And then there was Gina . . .

She reached out for the white phone beside Nick's bed and dialed Gina's number, but there was no answer, so she crawled out of bed and went to get dressed. The police station wasn't a problem, but Alan Sigler . . .

She spread her clothes out on the white bed in the guest room and stared at them in dismay. They were fine for the police, fine for the Foundation, fine for protesting, fine for going out for pizza, but for making an impression on Alan Sigler?

Okay, she could get by with her blue skirt. Nobody ever looked at skirts, anyway. But she had to have something classy on top. People looked at stuff like shirts and jackets and . . .

She put on her skirt and went back to Nick's bedroom and opened his closet.

It was just as she expected. Racks of beautiful shirts, gorgeous jackets. Of course, they were all white and black, but robbers couldn't be choosers. She pulled a white shirt off a hanger and read the label: Armani. "Figures," she said, and then stopped, remembering that Angela wasn't around to talk to. She'd have to go back to the apartment to look for Angela.

She shrugged the shirt on without thinking any more about it, rolling the cuffs several times. When she looked in the mirror, the shirt was beautiful but too big. It fell in soft folds around her, but it looked as if she was playing dress-up.

She went back to the closet and pulled out one of Nick's black vests and put it on. Better. Now she looked like Annie Hall with legs. If she put on earrings, she'd look feminine enough to get away with it.

She grabbed the twenty off the bed and went to call a cab and Gina one more time.

"YOU'RE LATE, Christine said to Nick as he breezed through the outer office and into his own. "Park left you the Welch file."

"Christine, I'm the boss." Nick dropped into his desk chair and pushed the Welch file to one side. "I'm never late. Your world revolves around me."

"Mr. Patterson called," Christine said. "He wants to have lunch with you."

"Not today," Nick said.

"You're kidding," Christine said, and Nick looked up at the expression in her voice.

"No, I'm not kidding. I'm busy. Call Annalise Donaldson and make an early lunch date for today at The Levee. Call Alan Sigler and make a dinner date for tomorrow at The

Levee. Find out who the landlord is at this apartment house—" he handed her a card "—and get him on the phone immediately. Then get me Thom Nordhausen at the Charles Theater for racquetball at two. That'll get me out of a long lunch with Annalise. Reserve a court." He stared at his desk for a moment. "What am I forgetting?"

"The law firm?" Christine said.

Nick frowned up at her. "Do you know what effect chlorine has on latex?"

"Not good," Christine said. "Don't do that again."

"Remind me to have my pool drained," Nick said. "Now go. I want those people yesterday."

She was gone before he finished the last word.

He leaned back in his chair and looked at the Welch file. Plagiarism.

Nick closed his eyes and thought. If it wasn't for the partnership, he'd be running as fast as he could away from Welch. If Tess was right about the earlier story—and Tess was invariably right about injustice, because she had an *instinct* for injustice—then this was going to be a huge tangle.

But it might get him partner.

Hell, he'd handled huge tangles before. It wouldn't kill him to undo another one. He thought about it for a few more minutes and then hit the intercom button. "Christine, I need to set up a dinner later this week with Norbert Welch. Get him for me, please, but I'll talk to him."

"You're on for lunch with Donaldson and racquetball with Nordhausen at three," Christine said. "I'm working on the Siglers. Ray Briggs is on line two."

"Who the hell is Ray Briggs?"

"Landlord."

"Christine, you are a wonder."

"I need a raise," she said.

TESS SPENT the entire morning at the police station, a lonely lunch hour in her old apartment waiting for Angela to come back and an hour in the afternoon with Alan Sigler in his paneled office, talking about education, the Decker Academy and the board.

"It's really up to the board now," he'd told her as he walked her to the door at the end of the meeting. "I'll give you my highest recommendation, but it's the board's decision. And they can't act until the end of the month. One of the old board members resigned, and we're still screening replacements, so we won't handle the staffing problems until the next meeting. Keep your fingers crossed."

"Thank you," Tess said, shaking his hand. "I really want to work at Decker."

"I know," Sigler said, clearly puzzled. "I'm not sure why, though. You don't seem the type to be impressed by prestige and money."

"I just want to teach," Tess said, omitting to tell him she just wanted to teach at the Foundation.

It wasn't really being dishonest. It was being tactful.

Maybe Nick was starting to rub off on her, after all.

She left the Foundation early to catch the bus home, and it dropped her off at the end of Nick's street at four-thirty. As she walked home, she absentmindedly computed how long it would be until he got home. An hour and a half at least. Maybe two. Not too long.

She let herself into the house and changed into her sweats, relieved to be out of hose and heels. Then she wandered about the house, afraid to touch anything, missing Angela and trying not to miss Nick. It wasn't a big house, but it was extremely white and it echoed and it seemed cold although the thermostat said seventy.

Not the kind of place Lanny would have built.

Now that's ridiculous, she told herself. This was not about Lanny. This was about . . .

Lanny. Lanny and the manuscript.

She kicked off her flats and went to the phone.

"Elise?" she said when her mother answered. "It's me."

"Tessie?" Elise's voice came over the wire, enthusiastic and vague as always, as if she was really glad to hear from Tess but couldn't quite remember who she was.

"Right, Tess, your daughter," Tess said. "How's Daniel?"

"Just fine, darling," Elise said. "He's out in the garden now. It's almost past canning season, but you know your father—he keeps going until the ground is bare. Are you all right?"

"I'm fine, but I need your help. Listen closely to this because it's important—do you remember Lanny?"

"Who?"

Tess was patient from long practice. "Lanny. Remember at the Yellow Springs commune the man who told the CinderTess story?"

"Well," Elise began doubtfully, "yes, maybe . . ."

"Big guy, brown hair, brown beard, one summer in Yellow Springs. After he left, you used to read it to me at night, remember?" Tess urged her. "It was on notebook paper. In turquoise fountain pen."

"A fairy tale?" Elise said. "With princes and speeches?"

"Right! *Great.* Do you still have the manuscript?"

"Of course not, darling." Elise said. "That was almost thirty years ago. Why would I still have—"

"Who would have it?" Tess asked. "This is important, love. Think."

"Well, I suppose somebody from the commune might. But really, Tess, you're making a big thing out of a fairy tale."

Tess pulled Nick's phone directory off the shelf under the phone and flipped to the blank lines on the back page. "I need names and numbers," she told her mother. "Anybody who might know something about Lanny and the manuscript."

"Oh, Tess, I don't know," Elise said. "That was a long time ago, and we're all over everywhere by now."

"All right. Start with the names you remember, and if you know where they are now, tell me."

Half an hour later, Tess had seventeen names and three numbers and a promise from her mother to try harder to remember the manuscript. "Although I don't see why, dear," her mother said. "It seems like a lot of trouble to go to for nostalgia. Especially when there are so many things that need fixing in the present. How did the censorship protest go?"

"Fine." Tess briefly contemplated telling her mother about Welch's plagiarism and then discarded the thought. Elise and Daniel would immediately organize a public protest, and as much as she'd like to see it happen, she had to admit Nick had a point. They had nothing to go on yet but her memories. She needed more people who remembered the story. And she really needed the manuscript. Which meant calling everyone on Elise's list and asking them if they knew anyone, and then asking those anyones if they knew anyone . . .

Nick was going to have some phone bill.

"I'll write soon," Elise was saying. "I want to send you some of Daniel's jam. It's really—"

"Oh, I've moved," Tess said. "My apartment was robbed, and it was too dangerous to stay there. I'm rooming with a friend until I find another place, but you can send anything to this address and I'll get it." Tess gave her mother the address and phone number. "I'll probably be here another week or two at least."

"Is this your friend Gina?"

"No," Tess said. "This is my friend Nick. The Republican. But it's okay. I'm not letting him corrupt me."

"Ooh, yes. I remember your talking about him. Are you sleeping with him?"

"Yes," Tess said.

"Is he good?"

Tess rolled her eyes, not really surprised. "Elise, that is no question to ask your daughter."

"Of course it is," Elise said. "Don't let conventional morality blind you to what's important in life. A satisfying sex life can be the foundation of a good relationship, and every mother wants her daughter in a good relationship."

"With a Republican?"

"Well, that depends on the man, dear. I met some very enthusiastic Republicans in my youth."

"I'm sure you did."

"Is he any good?"

"The earth moves nightly," Tess said.

"Well, then, I won't worry."

Five minutes later, Tess extricated herself from her mother's distracted conversation and called Gina.

"Hey, where were you this morning?" Tess said when Gina picked up the phone. "I called twice."

"I got it!" Gina said.

"Got what?"

"The job at the Charles Theater. And it's not a typing job. It's a good job. I'm a liaison! I didn't even know what that meant an hour ago, but Mr. Nordhausen explained it, and I'm going to be talking to people about the theater and making sure stuff gets done. It's wild! I've got a real job!"

"Gina, that's wonderful!" Tess sank onto the suede couch, oblivious to the furniture in her relief. "Let's celebrate. We'll go out and—"

"I can't," Gina said, her voice growing even more effervescent. "Park's taking me out! I called him and told him and he was really happy, and he said we should go out and celebrate. We're even going out tomorrow, too, so I can tell him about my job after the first day!" Her voice dropped a notch. "I probably shouldn't have called him but—"

"You called Park already?"

"I know, I'm pushing it, but I wanted him to know," Gina said. "We talked about it all weekend, and he told me what to do in the interview and what to wear and everything. I wanted him to know, and he was real happy and said we should go out. And we're going out!"

The happiness in Gina's voice was so blatant that Tess lost her breath. *Don't fall for him,* she thought, but all she said was, "That's wonderful, Gina. When do you start?"

"Tomorrow!" Gina said. "Can you believe it? Mr. Nordhausen was late at first because he'd been playing racquetball, and he came in all tired. I could tell he wasn't very keen on me at first, but then we started talking and I actually knew a lot of the theater people he kept mentioning, and by the end of the interview he said he wanted me to start right away—that I was just what the Charles Theater needed, after all."

"After all?"

"Yeah, I thought that was strange, too, but what the hell, I got the job." Gina's voice rose even higher. "I did the interview and he liked me and I *got* the job!"

Tess laughed at Gina's enthusiasm. "And you are going to be *great* at it. You're the best thing that ever happened to Nordstrom."

"Nordhausen," Gina said. "Hey, where are you? I called your apartment, but the phone company says your phone is dead."

"My whole apartment is dead," Tess said. "It got vandalized. I'm staying with Nick."

"Oh," Gina said. "How's Nick?"

"Nick's fine. The house is a little...well, I guess it's just not really my kind of house."

"Don't tell me. Let me guess. It's too expensive and successful-looking. Come on, Tess. Enjoy it."

"It's not that," Tess said, looking around. "I think you have to see this place to understand. To start with, it's totally black and white."

"No color?"

"None. I swear, I'm going to dig my old sofa pillows out of my duffel and put them on these couches just so I know I'm not color blind." With a start she realized she was sitting on the couch and slid to the floor. "Not that I'm ever going to actually sit on the couches."

"Why wouldn't you sit on the couches?"

"They're white suede."

"You are kidding me." Gina hooted with laughter. "This I gotta see. Okay, he's got suede couches. What else is wrong?"

"Well, nothing. I mean, he's darling to me, and he makes love like a god, and I'm safe and warm..." She looked around the icy splendor of Nick's living room. "Well, fairly warm."

"You don't sound sure," Gina said. "If he was the right guy, you'd be sure." Her voice sounded sure, and that made Tess's heart sink. *Not Park*, she thought. *Please, not Park.*

"So let's get serious about this," Gina said. "I want you to be happy, too. What are you looking for in a man? And why hasn't Nick got it?"

Tess stopped to think. "Actually I'm not really looking, but if I was..." She smiled to herself a little wistfully. "Well, with the manuscript and everything I've been thinking a lot, and I guess I want somebody like Lanny."

There was a long silence before Gina said, "Did you ever think that maybe not even Lanny would be Lanny today? Maybe he'd be Nick."

"That's ridiculous," Tess said. "Lanny would be..." What? She couldn't imagine Lanny in the nineties. He was permanently preserved in the golden sunlight of the sixties, like a fly in amber. "You know my life was a lot easier when everything was black and white," she told Gina.

"Maybe that's why Nick decorates like you think," Gina said. "Listen, I gotta go start getting ready. Park's not picking me up till late, he has to work or something, but I want to look spectacular!"

"You already look spectacular," Tess said, but she felt numb as she listened to Gina's ecstatic goodbye. *Please don't let her get hurt*, she prayed, but she knew it was a forlorn hope.

8

AT SEVEN, Nick came home with Chinese takeout and Angela.

Tess ran downstairs to meet him when she heard the door open. "Gina got the job! And I made a lot of long-distance phone calls—" Tess began. Then she saw the cat. "*Angela?*"

"I stopped by your apartment and there she was," Nick said as she pulled the cat out of the deluxe carrier he'd bought for her. "Damnedest thing."

"Right." Tess hugged Angela to her. "How much did you give Stanley to find her?"

"Not that much," Nick said. "I got Chinese. A double order of pot stickers."

"I'm crazy about you," Tess said.

Nick blinked, looking surprised and pleased. "Yeah?"

Tess buried her face in Angela's fur. "Yeah."

"Good. Hold that thought." He looked down at her clothes. "You know, I really hate those sweats."

"Don't start," Tess said. "I'm feeling affectionate."

"What sweats?" Nick kissed her, and she leaned against him until Angela showed her disapproval with her claws. "Lose the cat," Nick said, and moved into the dining area. He dumped the bags on the table and started taking out cartons. "That's great about Gina. Now, what was that about phone calls?"

Tess trailed after him. "I've started looking for Lanny and the manuscript. So far, I've got nothing, but I've got a couple of hot leads for tomorrow."

"Okay." Nick was obviously not enthused, but he didn't push the point. "Is there anything I can do to help? Christine can make some of those calls for you, if you'd like."

Tess dropped into a chair and pulled a carton toward her. "Who's Christine?"

"My secretary." Nick grinned. "Hell of a woman, Christine."

Tess stopped, her fork frozen in midair as she scooped pepper steak from the box. "Is she?" she asked coolly.

Nick's grin widened. "You're jealous." He collapsed into the chair across from Tess, beaming. "My life is now complete. Pass the pepper steak. I'm a happy man."

"I'm not jealous," Tess said stiffly. Then she put down her fork and slumped back in her chair and grinned back at him. "Yes, I am," she said. "All right, if I'm going to be a jealous bitch, I'm going to do it right. Tell me everything about her, and I'm warning you, she'd better be eighty-eight and ugly."

"She's a brunette, about thirty, and she's very good-looking." Nick stopped to consider what he'd just said. "She's just not very . . . human. She's like one of those models in the magazines, the ones who look as if they're having an out-of-body experience. Sort of . . . blank but still conscious." He shook his head. "She really is good-looking if you can get past the blank part. Park's been trying to date her since I hired her three years ago."

Tess thought of Gina and her grin evaporated. "Is he still trying?"

"I suppose so." Nick was so busy with the rice that he didn't see her frown. "It's not going to do him any good. Christine does not date her bosses."

"And how did you find this out?" Tess asked, torn between protecting Gina and killing Nick.

"I asked her out," Nick said. He scooped up some rice and then paused with the fork halfway to his mouth as he caught her glare. "Three years ago," he added. "I asked her out three years ago right after I hired her. I didn't even know you then." When Tess's scowl didn't fade, he put down his fork and addressed her with great patience. "That was three years ago, Tess. And now I think of her as a sister. An extremely attractive, extremely efficient, extremely distant, extremely platonic sister." He picked up his fork again. "This jealousy thing is a real ego trip for me, but don't overdo it."

"Do you ever get jealous of me?"

"No," Nick said. "You are the straightest person I know. You'd never cheat on me." He went back to his pepper steak.

"What about people from my past?" Tess asked him.

"Like who?"

"Like Lanny."

Nick choked on his rice and steak, and Tess handed him a paper napkin. "Lanny?" he said when he recovered. "I thought you said—"

"Gina and I were talking and I started thinking I might be using him as a sort of...ideal," Tess said. "She made me think that might be why I'm so hard on you all the time. Because you're not Lanny."

Nick pushed his food away.

"Don't stop eating," Tess said. "It's just a dumb theory."

"This Lanny. He was a big guy with brown hair and a brown beard and Abraham Lincoln ears, right?"

"Right. How did you know about the ears? I'd almost forgotten that." She leaned forward. "Did you find a picture?"

"No," Nick said. "I guessed."

"You did not." Tess pushed her own food away. "You did not guess big ears. You—"

"I guessed that because every one of those losers you've dated since I've known you has been a big guy with brown hair and big ears," Nick said. "I used to wonder where the hell you found them. I had one theory that they were cousins."

Tess's mouth dropped open. "My God. You're right."

"Two of them had beards." Nick pulled his food back in front of him. "So what does this tell us?"

"That I'm living in the past?"

"Maybe if I grew a beard . . ." Nick said.

"No," Tess said. "I don't want you to be Lanny. I love...the way you look."

Nick's head had jerked up on "I love," and he watched her for a moment before he said slowly, "All right. No beard."

"I've been thinking. I'm sorry if I was . . . a burden this weekend."

"You know that stuff you told me about how I turn into Dr. Jekyll and you hate it?" Nick said.

"Yes."

"Well, sometimes you turn into Crusader Rabbit and I hate it. But sooner or later, you're Tess again, so I just wait. Your dinner's getting cold. Eat."

Tess began to poke through the cartons, feeling ridiculously relieved about nothing in particular. "So where are the pot stickers?"

"You only get half, so don't even think about pigging out on them," Nick said, but he slid the carton across the gleaming ebony table anyway.

Tess watched him over the top of the carton as she fished out one of the dumplings. His shirtsleeves were rolled up and the muscles in his forearms flexed as he scooped out rice and beef, and that lock of hair fell in his eyes again. For once she was positive he didn't know about it. She ate slowly, listening to his voice as he talked about his day, automatically answering his questions about the phone calls she'd made and watching every relaxed move he made. This was Nick at home, shoes off, being completely himself, scarfing down Chinese food at the speed of light.

It was the sexiest thing she'd ever seen.

"I'll be right back," she said when the last of the pot stickers was gone. She went upstairs to the bedroom to get a condom out of his night table. Then she went back downstairs
and seduced him on the dining-room table with remarkably
little protest from him, although he did point out later that it
was a damn good thing he had expensive tastes in furniture
or they'd have ended up on the floor with some serious splin-
ter problems.

"I know, I know," Tess said, curled warm against him on
the table. "You'd rather be in a bed."

"Oh, I don't know." Nick reached over her to get a carton
that had toppled onto a chair earlier in the proceedings. His
body was hot against hers still, and she snuggled into him re-
flexively. He balanced the carton on her shoulder and fished
out a fortune cookie. "At least this way, I don't have to go
downstairs for the after-sex munchies." He offered her the
cookie.

Tess took it and broke it open. The fortune read, "You are
beginning a new journey."

"Well, that's true enough," she said, and rested her cheek
against his shoulder as he broke his open next to her ear.
"What does yours say?"

"People who make love on dining-room tables screw up
their knees," Nick read.

"That's not right."

"The hell it isn't," Nick said. "I may never walk again. I was
already wiped out from throwing three games of racquetball."

"Racquetball?" Tess said.

"Don't ask, it was awful." Nick sat up on the table and
rubbed his knee. "If you're really set on this table business,
I'm going to send Christine out for knee pads."

"Forget Christine," Tess said, and pulled him back down
to her.

The fortune cookies ended up on the floor this time.

"CHRISTINE?" NICK SAID into the intercom the next morning. "Come here. Your master calls."

Christine appeared in front of him, staring into space, probably planning a coup somewhere. He just hoped it wasn't at Patterson and Patterson.

"Christine, I have a lunch date today with Mr. Patterson," Nick began.

"I know. I made it."

"So I won't be able to take care of a little problem I have," Nick went on, smiling at her benevolently. "And I thought that since you did so well on the dress problem—"

"I get the afternoon off," Christine said.

"Done." Nick handed her a bag. "Replace these. Spare no expense. Then burn them."

Christine pulled a bleach-stained green sweatshirt out of the bag. "This is Tess's?"

"Yes. But not for long. Get rid of it."

"This is a mistake," Christine said.

Nick blinked. "You're disagreeing with me? You have an opinion?" He looked interested. "Christine, this isn't like you. Thank you for the input." His eyes dropped back down to his desk as he opened a folder. "Now, butt out," he said, dismissing her.

Christine dropped the bag on the desk with a plop, and Nick looked up, startled.

"I like you," Christine said with no expression whatsoever. "You're a good employer. You're simple, you're efficient, you're professional, and you're easy to manage."

"Simple?" Nick said, offended. "Simple, how?"

"Uncomplicated," Christine said. "Because of this I'm giving you some good advice, although it's my policy not to interfere in your personal life."

"Good policy," Nick said, but Christine kept on talking as if he wasn't there.

"Do not interfere with this woman's wardrobe," she said. "Clothes are important to women. She will resent it."

"Not Tess," Nick said. "Tess is incapable of carrying a grudge. Her attention span isn't that long. And she doesn't give a damn about her clothes. Replace the sweats and then burn them." He shoved the bag back over to her and turned to the work on his desk.

Christine picked up the bag. "This is a bad move."

"They're just sweats." Nick looked up again, annoyed, but she had already gone, doing her usual silent fade. "And get yourself some tap shoes while you're out," he called after her. "You're really giving me the creeps lately."

"Nicholas?"

Park's father appeared in the doorway. Tall and distinguished, with a patrician nose and a full head of gray hair, Kent Patterson looked like the perfect lawyer: wise, benevolent and just.

It was unfortunate that in reality he was a mindless, society-obsessed twit, but Nick had learned to deal with it.

"Kent!" Nick came around the desk to shake his hand. "I didn't think I'd see you until lunch, sir."

"Well, I'm afraid I'm going to have to cancel that, son," Kent said, clapping him on the shoulder. "Norbert Welch called me. Wants to talk contracts. Speaks highly of you. Good job there, Nicholas."

Nick felt his knees grow weak. "We got the account?"

"Not yet," Kent said. "But I'll be clinching that at lunch. Leave it to me."

Nick felt his knees come back. If Kent was in charge, they'd never see the account again. "Maybe I should join you, sir."

"Nonsense," Kent said. "You leave this in the hands of the master."

Well, I'm trying to, Nick thought. *But you won't let me.*

"You're free for dinner tomorrow, aren't you?" Kent asked.

"Of course," Nick said automatically.

"Well, that's good, because Melisande and I want to meet your fiancée."

"My what?" Nick said, appalled.

"Norbert told me all about her." Kent feigned a punch at Nick's shoulder. "You old dog. Kept her under wraps, haven't you?"

"Well, actually, sir—"

"Tomorrow at The Levee. Eightish. Just Melisande and I and Park and whoever he's dating at the moment—" Kent rolled his eyes derisively. "—and you and your...Bess, is it?"

"Tess," Nick said hollowly. "Me and my Tess. You bet."

WHILE NICK WAS DEALING with Park's father, Tess was dealing with her landlord.

"If there's anything you want, you just holler from now on," Ray Briggs told her. He stood on the front steps of the apartment building, his hands clasped behind his back over his ample rump as he swayed back and forth in his eagerness to please. His bald head gleamed through the six strands of hair he'd combed over it, and his normally mean little eyes had widened to the size of dimes in his efforts to look open and aboveboard.

It was so out of character for him that Tess was almost speechless.

"Well, actually I'm moving out, Ray," Tess said finally. "My furniture—"

"You give me the address. I'll have it all delivered," Ray said. "No problem."

"You're kidding. Well, all right. Now, about the locks—"

"First class all the way." Ray gestured to the door. "Here in front, on all the apartments, back door, too, just like the doctor ordered." Then he laughed asthmatically. "Or the lawyer, I guess, huh? Come on, check 'em out."

"Lawyer?" Tess said, but she already knew what had happened. She followed Ray through the building, checking to make sure that he really had replaced the locks, listening to grateful thanks from the tenants who assumed her protest had made them safe. When they were finally back at the front door again, she gave Nick's address to Ray and then went down the steps to catch the next bus.

"Tess?" Ray called anxiously.

She turned back. "Yes?"

"You be sure to tell Mr. Jamieson now."

Tess closed her eyes. "Count on it."

NICK CAME IN THE DOOR a little after six, stripping off his tie. "We're going out," he told Tess as he headed for the stairs. "Get your black dress."

"Hey," Tess said. "Wait a minute."

"Oh, right." Nick turned back, grabbed her and kissed her, swiftly at first and then lingeringly. "I'm still getting the hang of this roommate thing." He laughed in her ear as he held her close. "From now on, I swear I'll say, 'Hi, honey, I'm home.'"

"Good," Tess said, wrapping her arms around him more tightly. "This isn't actually what I meant, but I like it, so let's keep it." She kissed his ear. "I think that makes my line, 'How was your day, dear?'"

"Annoying as hell," Nick said, letting go of her and turning back to the stairs. "And we've got drinks at seven and a dinner date at—"

Tess grabbed his arm. "Not so fast, buddy." She pulled him over to the couch, pushed him down and then curled up beside him. "I talked to my landlord today," she began, absentmindedly rubbing her hand along his neck, just for the pleasure of touching him.

"God, that feels good," Nick said. He let his head drop forward. "Don't stop."

Tess began to knead her fingers into his neck muscles as she went on. "All the apartments have new locks. The tenants are very happy. Isn't that amazing?"

"Mmm." Nick let his shoulder slide down the back of the couch as she rubbed. "Do that harder."

Tess rolled to her knees so she could reach him as he slumped away from her. "So you called my landlord and threatened him with something ugly and legal, didn't you, Batman? Had to be a hero."

"Are you mad about this?" Nick mumbled. "Not that I care. Keep rubbing."

"No, I'm not mad. How was racquetball yesterday with Nordstrom?"

Nick's face was practically in a pillow by now. "Nordhausen. It was awful. Why?"

"You got Gina that job."

"Look, Tess—" Nick began, trying to sit up.

Tess pushed him back down. "You're my hero, you know that?"

"I am? Good. Keep rubbing."

"And that's why I'm going to put on black crepe and act like a Stepford wife for you and your career tonight," Tess said. She gave his neck one final rub and slapped him on the back. Then she stood up and headed for the stairs. "Who are we impressing tonight?"

"Drinks with Park and his date, dinner with Alan and Tricia Sigler," Nick said, his voice only partly muffled by the pillow. He moved slowly against the cushions and then slumped back down, evidently too comfortable to get up. "God, that was great. Let's get married and you can rub my neck forever."

"The Siglers?" Tess said, coming slowly back to him. "This is for me, not for the law firm?"

"Be nice to her tonight—your career is on the line," Nick said, still facedown in the pillows. "Could you do my neck again, just for a minute?"

"Possibly for the rest of your life," Tess said, sinking down beside him.

"What?"

"Nothing," Tess said, and went back to work on his neck, feeling an odd little glow take hold of her as she moved her hands across his muscles. It wasn't exactly sexual, but it was visceral, and she felt warmed by it and absentmindedly dropped a kiss on his neck in acknowledgment of it. *This isn't bad,* she thought. *This is good. This is comfortable.*

I like this.

The glow lasted all the way out of the house and into the restaurant bar where they were to meet Park and Gina.

Park was standing by the bar, as relaxed and handsome as a model in a liquor ad. But standing next to him was a brunette with blond streaks in her hair, and it took Tess a moment to realize that she was with Park, that she was Park's date and that Gina was still back at the apartment, waiting to be stood up.

"What's wrong?" Nick asked her.

"Say goodbye to Park," Tess said, making a beeline for the bar. "I'm going to kill him."

9

NICK GRABBED her arm and swung her around before she could get close enough to Park to attack him. "What the hell are you doing?" he whispered, dragging her to the other side of the bar as several people turned to stare.

"He's standing Gina up," Tess spat. "She's home expecting him to pick her up and he's with this . . . this . . ."

Nick closed his eyes. "Oh, hell."

"You're not surprised," Tess said, dumbfounded by the discovery. "I thought you'd be defending him, but you're not surprised at all."

Nick pushed her gently onto a bar stool and trapped her against the bar by putting a hand on the rail on each side of her. "I was afraid of this. Look, Tess, Park can't say no to anyone. He's a nice guy without much backbone. The one thing he is absolutely rock solid on is not defying his father. And his father will never buy Gina as any part of Park's life. So Park will not be seeing Gina. I'm sorry, it's lousy. I think Gina is a great kid, but there it is."

Tess sat rigid with fury. "I still want to kill him. He's going to hurt her. I don't care about his damn backbone. I still want to kill him."

"Well, you can't," Nick said. "You're in a public place. Control yourself. People are watching." He met her eyes and relented. "He didn't call her, did he?" he asked gently. "She called him. I'm not saying that makes it right, but Gina got the job and called him and said let's celebrate and he said sure."

"Oh, damn it." Tess blinked back tears. "I knew she shouldn't have called him. She's just so crazy about him she's transparent with it. She just couldn't wait." She pushed Nick away gently and stood up. "All right, I won't kill him in public. I'll call Gina tomorrow and see what I can do. Maybe if I introduce her to one of the guys from the Foundation . . ."

"Tess, you can't fix everything for everybody," Nick said, but his voice was sympathetic as he put his arm around her. "And this is between Park and Gina. It's none of your—our—business. Come on, we'll make this short so you don't have to look at him for very long."

"I want him dead," Tess said.

"I know," Nick said. "Try not to act on that."

The high point of drinks with Park and Corinne the brunette came for Tess when Corinne mentioned the amusing little gallery they'd had coffee in the night before. The night Park had told Gina they'd go out to celebrate her new job. Going out two nights in a row, Gina had marveled. Poor Gina. Stood up two nights in a row. All the lousy things Tess had ever said about Park came back to haunt her because they weren't lousy enough.

She glared at Park, who looked at her with equal parts of fear and confusion and immediately suggested to Corinne that they'd better be going.

"I want him dead," Tess repeated to Nick when they were alone, and Nick said, "I know. I know."

Dinner with the Siglers was only a slight improvement, although Tess was so despondent over Gina that she was actually polite and nonconfrontational.

"You behaved very well tonight," Nick said to her when they were on their way home. "The Siglers were impressed. I think Tricia is ready to forgive you for the roll fight." When Tess didn't answer, he glanced over at her. "Are you all right?"

"Gina," Tess said. "She's probably sobbing into her pillow right now."

"Do you want to drop by?" Nick said. "I'll wait if you need to be with her."

"No," Tess said. "Gina doesn't like crying in front of people. I'll wait until tomorrow when she's cried out, and then I'll do something." *God knows what,* she thought and slumped back into the leather of Nick's car seat while he drove her home in quiet, secure luxury.

THE NEXT DAY, Tess bought a five-pound box of hand-dipped chocolates and went to see Gina at work. She asked for Gina at the receptionist's desk, a walnut edifice that went well with the grimy marble floors and wainscoted walls and the wooden receptionist, who looked upholstered in her tapestry suit.

"Would this be theater-related?" the woman asked, staring suspiciously at Tess through horn-rimmed glasses. Tess was obviously not the sort of clientele she was looking for.

"It definitely has dramatic potential," Tess replied, and the receptionist waved her to a door down the hall, craning her neck to watch her go.

At Gina's door, Tess took a deep breath and then went in, smiling, determined to raise Gina from the pit of despair.

"Tess!" Gina beamed and leapt to her feet and came tripping out to greet Tess, throwing her arms around her and hugging tight. "This is my office! Isn't it great? Isn't life wonderful?"

"Absolutely," Tess said, refiguring the pit-of-despair part of her plan.

"Candy?" Gina said, spotting the huge box.

"Uh, it's an office-warming gift."

"Just like Park," Gina said happily. "He sent flowers. Look!"

Park had indeed sent flowers. A dozen red roses bloomed on the desk, a dozen pink roses glowed on the filing cabinet, a dozen white roses and a dozen yellow roses crowded the worktable, and a dozen peach roses graced the bookcase, each in its own crystal vase.

"He said he didn't know my favorite color, so he sent them all. He said I could just throw out the ones I didn't like," Gina said, surveying her luxurious garden with pleasure. "I told him I loved everything he gave me."

"Oh," Tess said, sinking into a chair.

"We had dinner at this little Greek place the night before last, to celebrate," Gina babbled on. "And he held my hand. Can you imagine? It was so romantic."

"The night before last?" Tess asked in disbelief. "Are you sure?"

"Yes," Gina said. "It was late because he had to work late, but that just meant we were the only people there. It was so private and so romantic—"

"Late," Tess said. "How late?"

"He picked me up at ten-thirty," Gina said. "And then last night, he didn't get to my place until eleven, and he wanted to go out, but I talked him into staying in." Gina got a dreamily lascivious look in her eye.

"Last night?" Tess said, now really confused. Then the look in Gina's eye hit her. "Oh, no, you didn't?"

"It was wonderful," Gina said, dropping into her chair. "He's an absolute gentleman, even in bed."

"Great," Tess said, but she thought, *Great, he cheats on her* and *he's boring in bed. I am going to kill him.*

"He is so sweet to me, Tess," Gina said. "And he's so much fun. And I feel so good around him."

"Great," Tess said. The correct thing to do was probably tell Gina about Corinne, but she couldn't do it. Gina was too happy. She was just going to have to kill Park slowly, using her bare hands, and then Gina could mourn her loss without being humiliated by betrayal. "Great," Tess said again.

The receptionist poked her head in the door, radiating superior disapproval. "You've left your intercom off again, Miss DaCosta."

Much to Tess's surprise, Gina didn't cringe. She just leaned over and flipped a switch on the intercom. "There you go, Pamela," she said.

Pamela sniffed. "Call on three."

"Who is it?" Gina asked.

"I don't know," Pamela said, staring insolently at Gina.

Gina stared her down.

Pamela sniffed again and said, "I'll ask," and then slammed the door shut.

"Hello," Tess said, amazed. "What was that? Gina DaCosta the Terminator?"

"Park taught me that," Gina said, grinning. "He met her yesterday when he picked me up for lunch, and he told me she was going to make my life hell unless I handled her. Then he spent the lunch coaching me on handling her. You wouldn't believe what a great impression he does of her."

"Lunch, too," Tess said.

"I told you. He's wonderful."

Pamela stuck her head back in the door. "It's Mr. Patterson," she hissed, her cheeks flushed with excitement. "You're keeping Mr. Patterson waiting."

"Thank you, Pamela," Gina said. "But next time, use the intercom."

"Oh," Pamela said. "Right." She backed out the door, closing it quietly this time.

"You are not a nice person," Tess told Gina. "Keep up the good work."

But Gina was already on the phone, beaming as she listened to Park.

"I can't stand this," Tess muttered. She waved to Gina as she got up to leave, stopping only to liberate two dark-chocolate turtles from the box of candy as she went.

She left the rest of the five pounds of chocolate for Gina. She was going to need it.

DINNER WITH the Pattersons was not amusing.

Tess had never liked The Levee. She wasn't sure whether it was because all the waiters looked like Donny Osmond and acted like Prince Philip, or if it was because the decor was faux mint marble and real peach linen, or if it was because the menu read like a bad Martha Stewart special.

However, all of that paled beside the company she was keeping.

Kent Patterson was well built and graying, a man of distinction who knew he was a man of distinction. Several people genuflected when he walked into the restaurant and not all of them were waiters. The headwaiter called him by name. He returned the favor. The headwaiter swooned.

Melisande Patterson was not well built. She was skeletal and dry, like scorched paper, tanned to the point of leather, lifted and tucked until she looked like a mummy with platinum hair. Her suit was Chanel, and all she was missing was a Just Say No to Everything button. She surveyed Tess through her lashes and then looked away, as if the sight was too painful to bear.

"Get me out of here," Tess said under her breath, but Nick pressed her forward.

"Kent, Melisande," he said. "I'd like you to meet Tess Newhart. Tess, this is Kent and Melisande Patterson. The Pattersons have been like parents to me."

"It's been our pleasure, son," Kent said heartily. He took Tess's hand. "So here's the little woman we've been hearing about."

"I'm five nine," Tess said, and Nick kicked her on the ankle.

"How amusing," Melisande said, obviously not amused, and before Tess could retort, Park joined them with his date and they all sat down.

Corinne, of course, not Gina.

Tess drew a breath before she spoke to him, and it sounded like a hiss.

"Park!" Nick said hastily. "Great to see you. You're looking lovely, Corinne."

"Corinne always looks lovely," Kent said. "Always has." He beamed at her and patted her hand, and Corinne smiled wanly back, too reserved for emotion. "I remember when you were just a little slip of a thing, going to Miss Windesham's with Park. Couldn't have been more than five or six." Kent fawned over her paternally. "Always wanted a daughter just like you. Of course it's not too late to have a granddaughter just like you, is it, Park?"

"No," Park said miserably.

"But there's no need to rush into anything, either, is there, Park?" Melisande said evenly.

"No," Park said, even more miserably.

Corinne seemed oblivious to the byplay but Tess was appalled. She turned questioning eyes on Nick, but he just shrugged. Evidently this was business as usual for the Pattersons. If Park hadn't been such a son of a bitch, she'd have felt sorry for him.

"Corinne went to Radcliffe," Melisande said to Tess, turning her fire to a new opponent now that Park was cowed. "We're both alumnae. Where did you matriculate, Miss Newhart?"

Tess fought back the impulse to ask incredulously, "Somebody gave you a degree?" and smiled, instead. "Ohio State," she said. "Liberal arts major."

"Oh, a state school." Melisande smiled archly and then looked at Nick, raising her eyebrows at him.

"Yes, a state school," Tess said. "That's why they call it Ohio State, instead of Ohio Overpriced and Pretentious." She moved her ankle before Nick could find it with his foot.

Melisande blinked, and then Nick said, "Tess is a teacher. She's thinking about joining the Decker Academy."

"Teacher?" Corinne blinked at Tess. "You're a teacher?"

"Yes," Tess said gently, having nothing against Corinne except the fact that she existed. "What do you do?"

"Do?" Corinne repeated, confused, and Tess let it drop. The sad fact was that Corinne was perfect for Park. Neither one of them had ever had a coherent thought in their lives. And there was Kent, campaigning for incoherent grandchildren. It would be interesting to see who was going to win, Melisande or Kent. Whoever it was, it wasn't going to be Park, and Tess felt a stab of sympathy for him. He was a rat, but he was a trapped rat.

Poor Gina.

"So you work for a living," Melisande said. "How amusing."

Tess opened her mouth to say something rude and then glanced at Nick. He sat beside her, his face resigned to having his career skewered, and she suddenly felt guilty. It wouldn't kill her to behave, to help him out. He'd not only helped her out, he'd saved Gina, the other tenants and Angela. *Stop being such a pain,* she told herself. Then she turned to Melisande and smiled. "Yes. It's very amusing. Almost like volunteer work. Do you volunteer, Mrs. Patterson?"

"Why, yes." Melisande blinked in surprise and then happily went into a lengthy discussion of the tribulations of organizing the annual Opera Guild open house. Tess nodded appreciatively at appropriate moments, and then, as the waiter brought the first course, Nick leaned forward.

"Thank you," he whispered in her ear, and she shuddered with pleasure at the warmth of his breath.

"You deserve this," she said. "Thank you. For Gina's job and Angela and everything."

"My pleasure," he whispered back, and then he turned his wholehearted fawning attention to Melisande.

Oh, hell, Tess thought, and then she, too, smiled back at Park's mother.

It was only for one night. What could it hurt?

BY FRIDAY of the following week, Nick was feeling fairly confident. Tess had adapted amazingly well to his social life, he loved coming home to her at night, and Welch was giving every indication he was ready to sign the contract. Tess still wanted to kill Park, and Park knew it—her palpable animosity toward him every time he showed up with Corinne was making him a nervous wreck—but she was managing not to physically harm him. For Tess, that was a major move toward maturity. Nick had even managed to talk her out of telling Gina about Corinne. At the rate he was going, Tess would be civilized in no time.

Nick was pleased.

Of course, not everything was perfect. They'd been out every night for the past week—including two dinners with Norbert Welch—not getting home until after midnight, and while Nick was making social points and solidifying his career with an amazing amount of help from the reserved, newly well-dressed Tess, he was also too tired to make love. The good news was so was Tess—the strain of being calm and polite night after night took its toll—but somehow, that wasn't a comfort. Nick was grateful for her transformation into a dutiful wife-type person, but he was beginning to feel he might have lost something important.

And tonight, the one night they didn't have a dinner date, they were stuck touring an old house for the benefit of the Opera Guild. All he really wanted to do was stay home and have Tess rub his neck, but the Opera Guild open house was important to Melisande Patterson, so they had to go.

Then Tess was late getting home from tutoring at the Foundation, which infuriated him. She changed into a black mini and a flowing white shirt topped with a black vest. It wasn't until he helped her out of the car at the showcase house that he realized the vest was one of his Armani suit vests. He was fairly sure the shirt was his, too.

"You look very nice," he said tightly. "Feel free to wear anything in my closet."

"I do," Tess said. "Look, are you going to be mad at me for long? Because you knew I had to tutor, and I even left early to get to this stupid house thing so—"

"Don't start," Nick said grimly, and steered her to the door.

"Mr. Jamieson, how nice!" The starched matron at the door held out her hand graciously. "We were beginning to think you wouldn't make it."

"I wouldn't miss it, Mrs. Tate," Nick said. "I'd like you to meet a friend of mine, Tess Newhart. Tess, Mrs. Tate practically runs the Opera Guild single-handedly."

"Oh, nonsense." Mrs. Tate waved her hand and blushed and melted into a perfectly nice woman charmed by a perfectly nice man. Nick heard Tess sigh and looked over to see her smiling at him, acknowledging another snake-oil conquest, and he felt his own anger start to dissolve.

"It's my fault," Tess said to Mrs. Tate. "I was late getting home from work. Can we still see the house?"

"Oh, of course," Mrs. Tate said, beaming at her. "In fact, this is a good time. There's practically no one here now. You can take a nice leisurely tour."

"Oh, good." Tess leaned on Nick's arm and smiled up at him. "Let's see everything."

His heart warmed at her smile, and he thought about what life was like with her and what it had been like without her. And then he thought about how he was growing surer and surer that he never wanted to be without her again—no matter how exasperating she could be. Hell, he probably exasperated her some of the time, too. *Lighten up,* he told himself. *There's such a thing as taking yourself too seriously.*

"You look a lot better in that vest than I do," he told her, and her smile widened and washed over him.

"Well, that's what I thought," she said.

The last of his anger disappeared, and he followed her lead as they toured, helping her make lavishly demented plans for redecorating his house in green velvet, pink faux marble and purple gauze. She laughed and darted from room to room, and by the time they reached the fourth floor, the week they'd been celibate loomed large in his mind, and he wanted her so much he wasn't sure he'd make it home.

"I definitely think we should drape the bathroom in green velvet," Tess said at the top of the staircase. "It holds in the moisture so nicely." She leaned against him, and he put his arm around her and kissed her hair, and she laughed up at him, her eyes half-closed.

"Atmospheric," Nick agreed absently. If they left immediately, he could have her in his bedroom in twenty minutes. "Well, I think we've seen . . ." he began but Tess was pulling him along to the next door.

"Oh, Nick," she said, and he followed her in.

"Drapes again." He surveyed the walls that this time were swathed in thick white satin. "What is it with these people and drapery?"

"This looks like your place." Tess stood beside the black grand piano sitting solitary in the middle of the black-and-white-tiled floor and slowly turned around. The laughter was gone from her voice, and she seemed suddenly forlorn. "All black and white and empty."

"Well, not exactly empty." Nick watched her move through the room, her red hair floating like a fireball against the white satin. "There's the piano and you."

But Tess had stopped and was staring down at her clothes, appalled. "Even I match. My God, when did I start wearing black and white?"

"You look great," Nick protested. "And trust me, with that hair, you don't need to worry about black and white. You're always in Technicolor."

"Is this what you want?" she asked him suddenly. She spread her arms and looked down at her clothes. "Is this the way you want me to be?"

He stopped, taken aback. "I want you to be the way you want to be," he said, confused. "The way you've been since you moved in. You mean the clothes? You look great in black and white."

"That's not what I mean." Tess's face creased in concern, and she turned away from him to run her hands down the keys of the massive grand piano.

"Tess—" Nick stopped as she bent to look at something on the keyboard.

"I don't believe it," she said, disgust thick in her voice. "They've made this into a player piano."

"What?"

Tess spun around, indignant. "They've not only stripped all the color out of this room, they've stripped the people, too. You don't even need a pianist. Just flip the switch." She surveyed the room and then turned back to him. "I can't stand it anymore. I'm starting to be this room. You flip the switch and I act all dignified and cold." Her jaw clenched as she shook her head. "I don't want to be this room, Nick. This room needs some excitement in its life. And so do I." She walked to the side of the piano, and boosted herself up on the top, swinging her legs with sudden abandon and smiling at him evilly. "Come here."

"Are you crazy?" Nick said, equally appalled and aroused. "Get down from there."

"Come on, Nick." Tess stretched out full-length across the piano on her back, letting her arms dangle over the keyboard, and Nick tried hard to keep his mind off her curves and on the get-down-from-there part. "Let's strike a blow for humanity. Prove you're not a robot. Come over here and make love to me."

"Tess—"

"If you're worried about me destroying a great musical instrument," Tess said, tipping her head back to look at him upside down, "you can stop. Somebody already did that when they converted it. Can you believe they did that?"

"No," Nick said, distracted as she rolled over onto her stomach and kicked off her shoes. "What are you doing?"

Tess propped her chin on her hand. "Did you ever see *The Fabulous Baker Boys?*"

"Yes. With you. Get off that piano." Nick went to the doorway and checked the hall. There was nobody for miles, which relieved his mind considerably. Then he turned around to see that Tess was off the piano, which relieved his mind even more. But then she reached under her skirt and peeled off her black bikini underpants, which relieved him not at all. She tossed the pants at him, and he caught them.

"No," he said, feeling himself tighten as he watched her boost herself back up on the piano.

"How about *Pretty Woman?*" she asked him.

"*No.* Get off that piano." He looked down at the scrap of black lace in his hand and then crammed it into his pocket before it gave him any more ideas than he already had.

Tess crooked her finger at him. "Come here. We're going to reclaim this morgue in the name of human passion."

"No, we're not." Nick leaned in the doorway, trying to be cool. "Forget it. Get dressed. We'll go home. We can even stop and pick up a piano on the way if it's going to have this effect on you, but no, not here."

"Pretty please?" Tess touched her lips with her tongue and smiled at him from the piano, and he felt the heat turn his brain to mush.

No, no, no, *no*.

"No," he said, praying his voice was firm. "We can't. I don't have any protection and—" He stopped because Tess had slipped two fingers into her vest pocket and pulled out a condom. *"You planned this?"*

"Of course not," Tess said, dropping the condom on the piano. "But I've learned a lot from you. Forethought. Initiative." She batted her eyes. "Drive."

"Don't do this to me," Nick said, and then she began to unbutton her vest, and he went to her to stop her because somebody had to be an adult in their relationship.

He just hoped he could do it.

A little voice in Tess said, "This is really stupid," but it was drowned out by the louder voice that said, "You're turning into a Corinne clone. Break away now." The fear was real and so was the desire. She suddenly needed Nick's weight on top of her, needed the warmth and the love and the emotion that seemed so faraway in Nick's house when Nick wasn't with her—and sometimes even when he was. He was standing in the doorway looking at her with that Jekyll face again, and she wanted the real Nick back. The room was so cold, and the real Nick was so hot, and she wanted him.

So when he came to pull her off the piano, she leaned into him, running her toe up his inseam and loosening his tie as she moved her mouth softly to his neck.

"No," Nick said, trying to evade her mouth. "Come on, Tess, not here." He looked over his shoulder. "Anybody could come in here."

"Oh, please, Nick," she said against his neck, and he said, "No. Stop it."

Tess stopped moving her lips down his neck and rested her forehead on his shoulder in defeat. It wasn't going to work. She had to face facts: if she wanted Nick, it was going to have to be his way. And that meant not just making love in beds, but in everything. She suddenly saw a lifetime of proper dinner parties and Opera Guild open houses stretching before her, and the thought was so depressing her desire died.

"All right," she said, and slid off the piano to stand beside him. "Let's go home." Nick looked at her, his forehead creased with concern, and she tried to smile up at him. "It's all right. Let's go. I was being dumb."

He leaned down and kissed her gently. "You're never dumb," he whispered against her cheek, and then he kissed her again. This time his mouth was hot and sweet, and his tongue tangled with hers, and she felt the heat rise in her again. Then he put his arms around her, and she felt him hesitate as he realized that she didn't have a bra on. The hesitation was brief, then he moved his hands around to her breasts and she leaned into him, moaning a little as the pressure from his hands eased the ache there.

"Oh, don't," she whispered to him. "I want you so much I can't stand it."

He kissed her again, his mouth gentle against hers as he tasted her with his tongue. "I can't stand it, either," he whispered. "I'll never make it home." He put his hands on her waist and boosted her back up onto the piano, catching her mouth with his again.

"Nick?" she said when she came up for air, and he said "Don't change too much. I appreciate this week, but don' change too much."

As her relief turned to lust, she pulled him to her, wrapping her legs around him and taking his hand to move it under her shirt. His hand was cool on her breast, and she closed her eyes at the pure ecstasy of his touch, and then he pushed her back and rolled onto the piano with her. She moved against his weight and let her head fall back as he pulled up her blouse and took her breast with his mouth. His mouth felt so good and she wanted him so much.

Oh, yes, she thought as the familiar dizzying heat flooded her. Then he shoved her skirt above her hips and pulled her tight against him. She moaned and it was part laughter because it felt so good to be pressed against him after such a long, cold week, and because the cold, hard surface of the piano made the hot, hard weight of him even more exciting. Then his fingers were inside her, and she moved against his hand until she thought she'd die. She bit his shoulder through his jacket and clawed at him while he fumbled with the condom, and he muffled her moans with his mouth, and then he was inside her, and she didn't think at all anymore.

They fell back into the rhythm they found each time, and she felt herself winding tighter under him, felt herself about to explode, and then he stopped moving and put his hand over her mouth. She blinked in confusion.

"Mr. Jamieson?" Mrs. Tate called up the stairs for what was clearly the second time.

Tess's spurt of laughter was smothered under Nick's hand. "Yes?" he called back, giving Tess a warning glare that dissolved into a grin.

"Did you find the player piano?"

"Yes," Nick said. He was trying to keep his voice steady and Tess sympathized, she really did, but he was hard inside her and she couldn't bear it. She began to move against him, and he closed his eyes.

"Shall I come up and turn it on for you?"

"*No,*" Nick said. "Thank you, no. I'll do it."

Tess peeled his hand from her mouth. "The switch is on the left side of the keyboard," she breathed in his ear. "And then, if you don't mind, *please,* I think I could come if you'd get a move on." She rocked against him again and her voice broke. "I was *really* close before you stopped to chat."

"I have lost my mind," Nick whispered in her ear. "And it's your fault. But what the hell." He reached his arm over the keyboard, fumbling for the switch, and she shuddered as he shifted inside her. Then the piano leapt to life playing the Minute Waltz and Tess laughed out loud and Nick rocked against her until everything came free inside her and all her worries went out into the universe with any other rational thought she might have had.

"That was incredible," she told him later, when they were curled up in bed together. "That was the best."

"I knew I should have told Christine to get me knee pads." Nick winced as he stretched out his legs under the covers. "I'm too damn old for this."

"Ha," Tess said, and set about convincing him that he wasn't that old.

10

THE NEXT DAY Tess stomped past Pamela the receptionist to poke her head into Gina's office, meaning to stay only long enough to find out if Gina was still all right and still oblivious to Park's two-timing. She waved to her, and Gina, listening to somebody on the phone, waved back.

"I've only got fifteen minutes until the next bus," Tess whispered. "I just stopped by to tell you..."

But Gina motioned her in, and Tess gave the next bus up for lost and sat down in the chair across from Gina's desk.

"Thank you very much, Mr. Edelstein. I'm sure that will be satisfactory," Gina said in the well-modulated tones of an evening news anchor.

Tess gaped.

"Certainly. I'll be looking forward to that. Until then." Gina hung up and turned to Tess. "So what's new with you?"

"With me? When did you turn into Diane Sawyer?"

"The voice or the suit?" Gina asked, and Tess realized that Gina's usual black jersey separates were now lipstick red wool-crepe separates.

"My God. What happened to you?" Tess asked, staring at Gina's clothes.

"I'm taking voice lessons," Gina said. "I never had a speaking part, so I never needed them before now."

"And now you've got a speaking part?" Tess said grimly. "Like playing Park's girlfriend?"

"This isn't Park's idea," Gina said. "I was gonna...going to do this, anyway. It's important in my job. I spend a lotta...lot of time on the phone. I need this."

"And the suit? That helps you on the phone, too?"

Gina stroked the rich fabric of the sleeve. "Park bought me the suit. He said he liked me in black, but he bet I looked spectacular in red. So we picked it out together. It was so much fun."

"I bet," Tess said, consigning Park to the lowest level of hell for trying to stifle his guilt with his checkbook.

"Is it bad that I let him buy it?" Gina asked. "I love this suit. I wanted this suit. It's not like he's keeping me." She stuck out her chin. "And I do look spectacular in red. I don't know why I didn't dress in colors before."

"You look great," Tess said quietly.

Gina slumped back in her chair. "You don't think I should have taken the suit."

"No," Tess said. "That suit is none of my business. I was just thinking how much Nick would love it if I loved the clothes he bought me the way you love that suit. I didn't tell you, did I? He did it again. Like that black dress. Only this time he stole my sweats and replaced them with these silk jersey things that slither. I told him not to, and he just patted me and now he keeps on doing it. My jeans are DKNY, my sweaters are all crewneck cashmere Ralph Lauren and my nightgowns are LaPerla." Tess made a face. "It's like *Invasion of the Body Snatchers*. The stuff is beautiful, but it isn't me. Everytime he does it, I tell him not to, and he just laughs and says I looked sexy in the new stuff."

"So relax and enjoy it," Gina said.

"Gina, I don't like the clothes he buys me. I'm not being politically correct. I hate the clothes. Crewnecks make me itch and I like sleeping in old T-shirts. They're comfortable. And I hate the way the damn house is decorated—it's like a meat locker with rugs. And I hate the Opera Guild. And I've been trying to be a good sport about all of it, but being a good sport is taking up all my time."

"So? What else have you got to do with your time?"

"Find Lanny," Tess said, and Gina groaned. "Listen, I've been making phone calls right and left and I finally got a great lead. One of Elise's friends from the commune told me that another of the commune members willed all his papers to the University of Riverbend library, and his papers included an oral history of the commune by different people who lived there in the sixties. I mean, this is a hot lead. I've been planning to go over there, but I've put it off every night so I could go with Nick to the theater or to dinner with Welch or to the River Clean-up Dinner, or to the Opera Guild open house or some other damn thing." Tess stared at her friend miserably. "The smartest thing I could do is move out, but then I'm afraid we wouldn't ever see each other because we're both so busy and we'd never make love on a piano again."

"I think I missed a step," Gina said. "About the piano."

"That's another thing that worries me," Tess slumped down miserably in her chair. "I'm starting to change. For example, I really thought conventional sex would be boring."

"Conventional sex?"

"You know, in a bedroom at night with the door locked. Missionary position. Lights off."

"Go on," Gina said. "I'm trying to follow this. Nick likes the missionary position?"

"Nick likes all the positions, as often as possible. Which is pretty fantastic, when you come to think about it."

"Good," Gina said. "What's the part about the lights off?"

"That was an exaggeration. But he prefers sex in a bed. He's *happier* in a bed. He *prefers* a bed."

"So do I," Gina said. "My back doesn't hurt, and I can roll over and go to sleep without having to move around."

"Well, that's the problem," Tess said. "As much as I hate to admit it, so do I. I mean, the other stuff is exciting, but it doesn't last as long because of the risk, and I don't get to touch him as much, and I'm really starting to prefer bedroom sex."

"This is not a problem."

"Yes, it is," Tess said. "I'm getting conventional. I'm losing my edge. I'm changing."

Gina scowled at her. "Will you stop it? You're not changing. Now, about this piano. Where exactly was it?"

"The Opera Guild open house."

Gina sat up straight. *"Are you nuts?"*

"You know, you sound a lot like Nick."

"There wasn't even a *door* on that room."

"How do you know?"

"Park took me on my lunch hour yesterday." Gina slumped back again. "I can't believe you lured that man onto that piano. He must be crazy about you."

"Oh." Tess stopped to consider it. "You're right. He must be. I hadn't thought of that. He was just standing there in the doorway looking like Jekyll, and I was afraid, so I—"

"So you tempted him into risky sex to make yourself feel better?" Gina's voice sounded disbelieving. "Have you any idea what would happen to his career if he got caught doing you on a piano at the Opera Guild open house?"

"I hadn't really thought about it," Tess said. "What would happen?"

Gina gave an exasperated moan. "Don't you pay attention to him? I can't believe you're this selfish."

"What are you talking about?" Tess said, insulted. "Of course, I pay attention to him."

"Then you'll have noticed how important his social life is to his career," Gina said. "You'll have noticed how often he's mixing with people and making connections. You'll have noticed what a great reputation he has in this city."

"Of course, I've noticed," Tess said. "I've spent the past two weeks of my life in that superficial social stuff."

"It's superficial to you," Gina said. "It isn't to Nick or Park. Or me."

"What?"

"I said, 'Or me.'" Gina looked at her defiantly. "I'm sorry. I've joined the dark side. Sue me."

Tess stared at the ceiling, speechless for a moment. "I don't believe this. How could you?"

"I don't believe *you*," Gina said. "I can't understand why you're so bigoted."

"Bigoted!" Tess said. "Me? I—"

"Listen, if I shaved my head or decided to become a druid or told you I was a transvestite, you'd be there for me, no judgment, no argument. But because I want to join the mainstream, you're going to bitch at me."

"Well, no. I'm just—"

"And every conversation from now on will be 'Gina, are you sure about this?' and 'Gina, you've been corrupted by wealth,' and 'Gina, if you'd just forget about Park and meet a nice guy with *values*' and—"

"Look," Tess said. "It's just that—"

"It's just that you don't respect me enough to respect what I want," Gina said. "I have to want what you want or it doesn't count or it's no good. And so does Nick and so does Park. Well, we don't want what you want. And I don't see why we have to. I mean, as long as we respect what you want and let you live your life, why do you care?"

"Because you're *changing*," Tess said. "I watch you when you're with Park. You're quieter and you don't talk as much and you dress—"

"I dress to fit in," Gina said. "And I'll tell you something. I like it."

"But you used to wear those...those..." Tess fumbled for the words. "You know, those dancer things. You were darling and avant garde and sexy. And now you look . . . I don't know. Adult."

"I dressed like a dancer because I was a dancer," Gina said. "Now I want to be an adult so I'm dressing like one. And when Park and I are alone, I talk. We talk all the time."

"But not in public." Tess seized on the point. "When you're out with Park—"

"I never have talked much in public," Gina said. "I'd rather listen. I've always been that way."

"You have? Then why haven't I noticed?"

"Because you were always talking," Gina said. "You talk. I don't."

"I still think you're changing because of Park," Tess said stubbornly.

"Okay, say you're right," Gina said. "So what?"

"Well, that's wrong. You've got to be yourself."

"I am myself. I'm just trying to be more like someone I care about. I'm adjusting. And why not? He's adjusting to me. He came over the other night and I made canned ravioli and he liked it. And last weekend I took him to the midnight showing of *The Rocky Horror Picture Show* and he threw toast."

"Park threw toast?"

"Change doesn't have to be bad, Tess. People write books about it all the time. Only they call it 'personal growth.'"

"I suppose," Tess said reluctantly. "I just think I could handle your personal growth better if it wasn't being inspired by Park."

"Tess, I love Park." Tess closed her eyes in pain, but Gina went on. "I know you don't like him, but I don't care. You don't know him. Underneath he's really sweet and kind and understanding, and I've never felt so taken care of in my life, and I want to give him the world and I'm going to, so just butt out."

Tess swallowed everything she knew about Park and smiled. Tightly. "All right. All right. I'm happy if you're happy."

"Really?"

"Really," Tess lied.

Gina sighed. "Well, then, to tell you the truth, I don't know if I'm happy or not. Park's wonderful, and when it's just us, everything is great, but sooner or later I'm going to have to meet his family, and I don't think I fit the profile of a Patterson wife."

"Me, either," Tess said. "But I've met them and I'm faking it. No reason why you can't, too." She shifted uncomfortably in her chair, knowing that she should be telling Gina the truth—that there was no way in hell that Park was ever going to introduce her to his family, that she was never going to have to fake it, that Park was two-timing her with a social X ray his father was already calling the mother of his grandchildren. Then she looked at Gina, serene and lovely and glowing, and she thought of Nick telling her to stay out of other people's lives, and she stifled herself. It might still work. Maybe. Maybe Park would fall in love, find a backbone, defy his father, and marry Gina.

Fat chance.

"Look, is there anything I can do for you here?" Tess asked, desperate to help with something small since she was obviously no help to Gina at all with the big stuff.

Gina looked at her sternly. "Yeah. Don't get Nick arrested for public indecency on a piano. It's bad for the firm."

"Oh, come on, Gina, it's not that big a deal."

"You know, you don't have to change completely in order to stay with Nick. You just have to understand his point of view."

"He had a very good time on that piano."

"Forget it," Gina said. "You'll never understand. Maybe you're right. Maybe you'd better move out. What with Nick trying to put you on the best-dressed list and you trying to put him in the Guinness Book of Records under Sex in the Dumbest Places, maybe you really are bad for each other."

Tess felt a chill. "Do you think so?" She bit her lip, feeling more miserable than before.

"If you're going to make his life hell, yes."

"So what you're saying is no more risky sex. What's the point in living if you can't take risks?"

"Work. Love. Children."

"Sounds boring."

"Then move out," Gina said. "You're just leading him on if you don't."

"I probably should," Tess said. "I've been there almost a month now. It's time."

Gina nodded. "Definitely."

"It's not like we're in love or planning a commitment or anything."

Gina shook her head. "Of course not."

"So I really should move out."

Gina nodded. "Absolutely."

"I don't want to," Tess said.

"I didn't think you did," Gina said.

"So HOW IS LIVING with Tess working out?" Park asked Nick at lunch at The Levee the next day.

"Great." Nick looked at him across the spotless linen warily. "Why do you ask?"

"Just curious," Park seemed distracted as he talked, absentmindedly crumbling a bread roll into dust. "I suppose there've been a few changes at your place."

"A few." Nick sat back from his empty plate. "But they're all good changes. Tess's clothes, for example. She dresses like Annie Hall on welfare, but I've been having Christine buy her new things and she looks great." He smiled, remembering how good Tess had looked in a midnight blue jersey the night before. "And the next thing that's going is that damn navy blazer," he added, his voice thick with satisfaction.

"She's been sort of . . . odd at dinner," Park said. "Quiet. Dignified. Is she sick?"

"No," Nick said, patient to the end. "She's trying to help me with my career."

"Oh." Park considered Nick's comment and shrugged. "Well, it's working. I think the only reason Welch is paying any attention to us at all is Tess. He never takes his eyes off her."

"I know." Nick frowned, remembering. "The old goat."

"What?"

"I know we want the account," Nick said. "I just don't like him leering at Tess."

"He's not," Park said.

Nick frowned again. "Sure he is. He—"

"No. I don't know what it is he sees in Tess, but it's not sex."

"Oh?" Nick sat back and surveyed his friend. "And how do you know this?"

"Because he never looks at her body," Park said. "Face it, most guys are either breast or leg men, and Tess does pretty well in both categories, but he never looks at anything but her face." He frowned, considering. "It's like he's looking for something or waiting for something."

Nick blinked. "You're right. I hadn't thought about it, but you're right. What is it?"

"I don't know," Park said. "And I don't care as long as it gets us the account." He shifted in his chair and started mutilating another roll. "Did I tell you about that new paralegal I interviewed? Very hot. I think I may ask her out."

Nick folded his arms and stared at Park with exasperation. "Park, what the hell are you doing?"

Park started and dropped his roll. "What?"

"This thing with Corinne at seven and Gina at eleven. And now a new paralegal." Nick looked at him sternly. "This is not good."

"How'd you know?" Park said, stunned.

"Tess talks to Gina," Nick said. "Have you lost your mind?"

"Yes," Park said glumly.

Nick rolled his eyes and leaned forward. "Park, you can't go on like this. I don't want to interfere, God knows I don't, but you have to stop this."

Park winced. "I know I have to drop Gina. I know that. It's just she's so happy—"

"Oh, for crying out loud." Nick threw his napkin down on the table in disgust. "You can't please the whole world. And I'm warning you, I can only keep Tess from blowing the whistle for so long. She wants you dead now."

Park was appalled. "She'd tell Gina?"

"Of course she'd tell Gina," Nick said. "Damn it, Park, let Gina down as easy as you can, but stop seeing her. What you're doing is cruel." He looked at his friend in puzzlement. "This isn't like you."

"I know," Park said. "I know. I'll do it. Soon. I really will. I can't stand this much longer, anyway. It's driving me crazy. I sit there with Corinne drinking champagne and then I go to Gina's and it's like I'm in a different world. Ravioli. Throwing toast. Watching a twelve-inch TV. Not what I'd expected."

"What are you talking about?" Nick said, totally confused.

"Nothing." Park shrugged. "Forget it. It's over. I knew it would be. I've just got to tell Gina and...and..." He stopped, unhappy and disoriented, and began shredding the roll again. "Oh, hell. Forget it. Women are hell. I don't know how you're still sane after four weeks with Tess."

"Sane? I'm not." Nick relaxed against the back of his chair, glad to be off the subject of Gina. "Did you ever live with a woman you found it impossible to say no to?"

"Yes," Park said gloomily. "My mother."

"This is different," Nick said. "We made love on the piano at the Opera Guild open house."

Now Park looked confused. "Why?"

"Because it was there," Nick said. "I don't know why. Tess said, 'Let's,' and I said, 'No,' and we did it." He shook his head. "We're going to get arrested one of these days, but it will be worth it."

"So that's what's keeping you with this woman? Great sex on pianos?"

"No," Nick said. "But it's not hurting the situation any."

"If she's what you want . . ." Park said doubtfully.

"She's what I want." Nick pushed back his chair and stood up. "Enough about me. Get rid of Gina before Tess tells her what you're doing and then dismembers you."

"Right," Park said. "Get rid of Gina."

AT ELEVEN-THIRTY that night, Tess came out of the history stacks at the university library to find Nick asleep with his head on a table.

"Nick," she said softly, shaking him. "Nick, honey, I'm sorry."

He shook his head a little to clear it. "It's all right. Did you find anything?"

"No," Tess said miserably. "Not one mention of Lanny anywhere. I swear I didn't make it up."

"I know you didn't." Nick rubbed a hand over his eyes. "You ready to call it a night?"

"How do you know I didn't?" Tess asked.

"Don't be ridiculous." He sounded testy as he pushed his chair away from the table. "You know I trust you. Of course you didn't make it up."

"Then why aren't you going to Welch?" Tess said exasperated. "Why can't you just talk to him about this? Why can't you talk him out of trashing Lanny? You're a lawyer. You can talk anybody into anything. And you know I'm never going to find that manuscript. It's hopeless."

Nick focused on her, slowly waking up. "You're giving up?"

Tess collapsed into the chair next to him. "I've talked to people who remember Lanny and people who remember the stories, but nobody has a manuscript and nobody remembers it well enough to quote it. I've got nothing." She waved her hand toward the stacks behind her. "This was my last shot. But nobody even mentions Lanny. Notes from fifty commune members and nobody mentions Lanny."

Nick frowned. "Why not?"

"What?"

"He spent the summer there," Nick said. "Why didn't anybody mention him?"

"I don't know."

"What does this file look like?"

Tess shrugged. "It's just a big folder full of papers."

"It's not bound?" Nick said. "Are the papers numbered?"

"I don't know. It—" Tess stopped when Nick leaned back in his chair and sighed. "What?"

He stood up and pulled her to her feet. "Come on. I'm going to hate myself for this, but show me this damn file."

Ten minutes later, Tess looked at the notes she'd made. "According to the log, four sets of papers are missing," she said. "All from the summer of 'sixty-five. One of them was a manuscript. Somebody took them out. Why?"

"We know why," Nick said, shoving the file box back on the shelf. "Somebody's trying to wipe out any evidence of Lanny. What we need to know is who."

The research librarian was furious when she found out that papers had been removed. She called up the computer file immediately, and then they watched as her fury turned to confusion. "This can't be right," she told them. "In the ten years that file has been there, only one other person has checked it out."

"And that would be?" Nick prompted.

She blinked at them. "Norbert Welch. Why would he vandalize an old oral-history file?"

"I have no idea," Nick lied, nudging Tess to keep quiet. "Thank you very much."

"The rat," Tess said as she followed him out of the library. "The lousy, cheating, plagiarizing, library-vandalizing rat."

"I know," Nick said. "I'll talk to Park and we'll figure what to do tomorrow." He caught her hand and pulled her along with him toward the parking lot, overriding her next question. "I don't know what we're going to do yet. And right now I don't care. I just want to go home and go to bed. I have to be in court first thing in the morning."

Tess started to protest his dismissal of Welch and then winced as the guilt hit her. He was tired and she was nagging him. *Don't you ever pay any attention to him?* Gina had asked, and here she was, totally oblivious to the fact that he had to get up early in the morning. He gave her the best of everything and she hated all of it, and now she was dragging him through libraries in the middle of the night so he could help her destroy his career.

If you had any consideration for this man, she told herself, *you'd get out of his life.* As a personal goal, it had very little appeal, but it was the right thing to do.

"Are you okay?" he asked when he'd walked her through the shadows of the parking lot and they were back in the car. He turned the key in the ignition, and the engine purred to life. "You're awfully quiet."

"I think I'd better move out," Tess said.

"What?" Nick turned off the ignition and faced her in the gloom, and she could hear panic in his voice. "What are you talking about?"

"I'm not good for you," Tess said miserably. "I don't look out for you and I'm going to ruin your career and—"

"Who the hell have you been talking to?" Nick said. "I don't need you to look out for me. *I* look out for me. And my career is fine. What are you talking about?"

"Yes, but suppose somebody had caught us on that piano?" Tess said. "Then where would you be?"

"Probably enshrined in the envious hearts of every man in Riverbend," Nick said. "Who started you on this?"

"I just thought that maybe you'd be better without me dragging you down into degradation every fifteen minutes."

"I like degradation," Nick said. "I've had more great sex since I discovered degradation with you than I'd ever dreamed of. Come here." He leaned across the stick shift and cradled her cheek in his hand and kissed her, and Tess melted into him, so grateful she wasn't losing him that she clutched at him and felt the swell of the muscles in his upper arm.

"I love you, Tess. Don't go," he whispered.

"I won't," she said, pressing her forehead against his. "I couldn't. Not really. Not anymore. I love you, too."

He kissed her again, and his mouth was hot, and every time she kissed him, she found the curve of his lips more dizzying. As she lost herself in the heat there, she let her hand trail lazily down his chest to the swell of his thigh and then between his legs. He drew in his breath sharply and his hand cupped her breast and she felt her breath catch, felt her blood shudder, and she wanted him, suddenly, now, any way, and she pressed against him harder, but he moved his hand away and said, "Oh, hell, Tess, not here."

11

TESS FLINCHED and pulled away. "I know, I know, it's the piano all over again. I'm sorry. This is exactly what I was talking about."

She moved away, trying to stomp down the need for him that was making her shake, but Nick reached for her and said, "No, that's not what I meant. There's a stick shift—there's no room." He kissed her then, and she fell back against him, suddenly desperate again, her tongue stroking his mouth frantically, needing some kind of release before she screamed. She trailed her hand down to open his zipper, and though he moved once to stop her, she stroked her cheek down his chest, feeling the curves and the hard muscle beneath his shirt before she took him in her mouth. His hand came to rest in her curls as she traced his length with her tongue, lost in the taste and the heat and silky smoothness of him until, after a few minutes, he pulled her head up again and kissed her, searching her mouth with his tongue.

"I need you now," she breathed, and he said, "I know," and kissed her again. Then he leaned over her and flipped open the glove compartment, pulled out a condom and flipped the compartment closed. His arm brushed her breast as he moved back and forth and she moaned at the touch.

"Steady," he said, and then a moment later he slid his hand down her back under her rear end, saying "Up."

"What?" she asked, but leaned forward, still dizzy with lust, and he maneuvered around the stick shift to slide into the passenger seat under her, pulling her hips against his from behind.

"Wait a minute," she said, and then she braced herself on the dashboard as his hands moved under her skirt to slip her underpants off and the heat of his hands on her thighs made her mute with need.

"You're the one who likes risk," Nick said from behind her, but his voice was laughing not angry. She felt him push hard inside her and her body arched in blissful spasm, and then he shuddered and said, "Oh, God, Tess," and she let her shoulders fall forward, trying to keep control and failing miserably.

Wait, she wanted to say. *I don't like it this way. I can't see you. I can't touch you. I can't taste you. I can't do things. I can't—*

But he had one hand under her sweater caressing her breast so gently she couldn't bear it, and the fingers of his other hand slid over her thigh and inside her and stroked in rhythm with his hips, and the heat kept blanking out her thoughts. She melted against him, forgetting why she didn't like it like this.

"Nick," she breathed, and he put his mouth against her ear and said, "What?" and his breath was warm and she felt herself start to go and clung to sanity with all her willpower.

"I'm not doing anything," she said, and it sounded weak even to her.

"For once, let me do it all," Nick whispered. "Just this once."

And she wanted to tell him she was a partner, a giver who was responsible for her own orgasm, but he felt so good and she couldn't speak anymore, anyway. Then she felt the hot chill start, and she moaned, knowing the spasms would come, and then just for an instant, with frightening clarity she realized she really didn't want to be responsible for her own orgasm this time. She wanted it to be all him, and then she relaxed into the wave, letting her head sink slowly onto her hands on the dashboard, as Nick rocked her into glorious oblivion over and over again.

"I CAN'T BELIEVE I let you do that," she said later when they were curled up together in bed. "I hate it from behind."

"You do not hate it from behind," Nick said sleepily. "They heard you come in Kentucky."

"This is scary," Tess said. "I can't say no to you."

"Tell me about it," Nick said. "I got laid on a piano."

"I'm serious," Tess insisted. "This was supposed to be just two really good friends sharing a good time and great sex and now I can't leave you."

Nick kissed a curl back from her forehead. "It was always more than that," he said. "You know it was always more than that."

"I really love you," Tess said, and his arms tightened around her and she shivered against him, grateful for his warmth.

"I love you, too," Nick said. "I think we should get married." She tensed in his arms, and he kissed her again until she relaxed. "Why not get married?" he whispered. "It's what we've got now."

"I'm not sure what we've got now." Tess shifted away a little. "I love you, I really love you, but living this way...I don't know. It's not me. I don't know."

"It's all right." He pulled her closer. "Just think about getting married. We can talk in the morning."

She could feel his body relax as he drifted into sleep, feel the weight of his hand resting comfortingly on her hip, but it was almost dawn before she fell asleep, too.

Tess followed him down to breakfast the next morning, groggy from lack of sleep as he zipped around the kitchen fixing himself toast and coffee and barking orders at her.

"Pick me up at the office at six," he told her, spreading jam on his toast. "I've got a late meeting, so catch a cab there instead of waiting at home for me."

"All right," Tess said tiredly. "Who are we wining and dining tonight?"

"The Pattersons and Norbert Welch," Nick said, and when Tess groaned he added, "Don't say anything about the papers at dinner. I'll suggest after-dinner drinks and then if Park agrees, we can talk to him. But no accusations, understand?" He pointed his toast at her to make his point before biting into it. "I want this contract, and we're about to get it. Don't screw it up."

"I know, I know, you'll make partner," Tess said, grumpy because she was so tired. "What I don't get is what difference can partner make? I mean, every single person we've been sucking up to for the past three weeks is crazy about you already. I don't see what partner is going to get you when Riverbend already thinks you're God in a three-piece suit."

Nick stopped for a moment, as if he was going to answer her, but instead he said, "You wouldn't understand."

"Try me," Tess leaned her head on one hand and yawned. "Give me one good reason why you need this."

"Okay," Nick hesitated again. "When I was eighteen," he said finally, "I was accepted at Yale. My dad was really proud. He'd put aside a college fund for me, but it wouldn't even get me a year at Yale. But he said no problem, he'd work extra overtime at the plant, and if he had to, he could tap into his pension, and with my partial scholarship we'd be all right."

"Sounds like a great guy," Tess said, waking up a little at the serious tone in Nick's voice.

"Then right before Christmas that year, my senior year, he got laid off. And because of the way things were run at the plant, he lost his pension. Then, three months later, still out of work, he lost control of the car and he and my mom died." Nick's voice had gone flat, and he finished his story with absolutely no expression. "He left nothing. Twenty-three years with the plant and he had nothing at the end. I still made it through. I'm okay. It's no big deal." He set his jaw and looked grimmer than Tess had ever seen him. "But all that work, a lifetime of work, and then he had nothing. It killed him." He met her eyes. "That's when I decided I was never going to work for anybody else. If I'm partner, I don't work for anybody else."

"Oh," Tess said.

Nick shook his head. "It's no big deal."

"Right," Tess said.

"Your toast popped. It's getting cold."

"I'm sorry," Tess said.

"No problem. Just put in a couple more slices."

"Not about the toast. About your parents."

"It happened twenty years ago, Tess," Nick said. "It's done." He got up to leave. "Don't go getting all weepy over it. I just want that security. For both of us. And for our kids. I don't want them ending up with nothing. So I am going to make partner, and nothing is going to get in my way."

"Kids?" Tess said. But he just kissed her goodbye, his lips lingering on hers a little longer than usual. She buried her head in his shoulder and clutched at his suit coat. "I love you," she whispered, and he said, "I know. I love you, too. Go back to bed. You're wiped out."

She sat at the table for a long while after he left, thinking about Nick and Nick's dad and the partnership that now was an understandable need. She ached for the Nick-at-eighteen who'd had his whole world ripped out from under him, but she ached more for the Nick-at-thirty-eight who was missing his life while he made sure the world would never get ripped out from under him again. And she suddenly realized that it wasn't just that he loved her, but that he needed her. She was his only hope for a real life, a life he could start having once he got that damn partnership. Once he got the partnership, he'd relax, and they'd be all right. He'd feel secure and he'd stop trying to impress people and he'd stop trying to change her. She could get rid of those damn clothes, Jekyll would disappear, and they'd be all right.

For the first time, Tess thought about marrying Nick without cringing. They were so right together. The only thing that kept them apart was his quest for success, and once that was satisfied . . . *marriage*, she thought, and pictured them together in this house. If they were married, she could insist on some color. Then she could come home from her jobs at Decker and the Foundation to a bright house and Nick and . . . their kids.

Kids. A boy and a girl because Nick liked symmetry. No redheads. Two neat little brunettes, like Nick. She'd have to keep them away from the pool—unless they took swimming lessons at the country club. Of course they'd take swimming lessons at the country club. They were Nick's kids. And the suede couches would definitely have to go—unless she raised them to be incredibly tidy, like Nick. And incredibly well behaved, like Nick. And of course, they'd have to go to the right schools and wear the right clothes and probably play the Moby Dick game, and as Tess visualized them in school uniforms, she suddenly didn't like them much.

Boring little twits, she thought. And then she thought, *Stop it.* It wouldn't be like that. Nick would change once he got the partnership.

Maybe.

It was too much to think about and she'd been thinking all night, anyway, so she went back upstairs and fell asleep and dreamed of dark-haired children who kept looking at her with contempt and saying, "Oh, *mother*," and Nick coming home and announcing he was running for president so she'd have to get new clothes. She didn't wake up again until three, when Gina called her, hysterical, because she'd just read in the paper about Park's engagement.

"How could he be engaged?" Gina said through her tears when Tess reached her apartment. "He's been with me every night. How could he have gotten engaged to somebody else?"

"Oh, Gina," Tess said, sinking onto Gina's moth-eaten couch and pulling her friend down with her. "Listen, honey, Park just . . ." She tried to think of a good way to put it, but the truth was that Park had been two-timing Gina all along and Tess hadn't done anything about it. "Park's a jerk," she finished. "So am I. I'm sorry I didn't tell you."

Gina pulled away. "You *knew*?"

"Nick told me not to get involved," Tess said miserably. "And I thought it might work out. You were so happy and . . . Oh, hell, I screwed up. I'm sorry. If you never forgive me, I understand."

"How long has he been seeing her?" Gina's eyes blazed at Tess. "How long?"

"I don't know," Tess said. "From the way his father talked, they've known each other since birth."

"He knew her before me?" Gina said. "So what was I? A fling? He knew all along that . . ." She stopped and swallowed. "And he didn't even tell me. He let me read it in the paper. Did he think I wouldn't care?"

"I don't know," Tess said. "I don't know what either one of them thinks. Sometimes I think they don't see us at all. They just see what they want to. Maybe Park thinks you're only looking for a good time. Maybe Nick thinks I enjoy being the new Nancy Reagan. I don't know. I just want to kill both of them right now."

Gina slumped back against the couch and picked up a pillow. It was a *Cats* T-shirt, plump with stuffing and sewn shut at the neck, sleeves and hem, and it looked oddly like a dismembered corpse as she hugged it. *That's what Park's going to look like when I get through with him*, Tess vowed, and then she concentrated on Gina. "Are you all right? Talk to me. What are you going to do?"

"I don't know," Gina said into the neck of her stuffed T-shirt. "I don't know. I love him."

Tess felt her whole body grow cold. "You are not going to see him again. Tell me you're not going to see him again. You wouldn't."

Gina's lower lip trembled. "I don't know."

"What do you mean, you don't know?" Tess stopped and tried to keep from shrieking. "He's getting married. What are you going to do? Be his understanding mistress? I know you're heavily into adapting your life to suit Park, but don't you think that's a little much?"

"Stop it, Tess," Gina said tiredly. "No, of course I'm not going to be his mistress. I just have to think about this. I'll have to give back all the stuff he gave me, and then . . . I don't know. I guess I don't want to see him."

"I guess you don't," Tess said. "My God, I guess you don't."

"Do you suppose Nick would pick the stuff up after I've packed it?" Gina asked. "Would he give it to him?"

"Of course he would," Tess said. "Whether he wants to or not. You don't ever have to see that rat again."

"He's not really a rat," Gina said. Then she sniffed. "Well, maybe he is."

"I'm going to kill him," Tess said, standing up. "I'm going to go get us ice cream and mashed potatoes and gravy and enough chocolate to coat Riverbend, and when we're done sedating ourselves with food, I'm going to tear that bastard apart with my bare hands."

"No, you're not," Gina said, her voice exhausted. "Just let him be. It's not your problem. It's my fault. I should have known better. What did I think he was doing with somebody like me, anyway?" She looked up at Tess. "I really thought he loved me. I really did. Isn't that dumb? No wonder I never graduated from high school. No brains."

Tess sat down again and wrapped her arms around Gina, holding her tight. "Stop it," she said. "Just stop it. This is his fault, not yours."

Gina buried her head in Tess's shoulder. "Don't worry about it," she said, her voice muffled. Then she pulled her head back and looked at Tess. "It's okay. I told you. It's not your problem."

Tess swallowed the lump in her throat that formed every time she looked at Gina's tear-ravaged face. It might not be her problem, but it was going to be her pleasure when she found Park, the son of a bitch. "What kind of Häagen-Dazs do you want?" she said, and went to work dragging Gina back to mental health.

Two hours later, Tess stormed into the outer reception area of Patterson and Patterson looking for blood. Park's blood. Splattered all over the walls if possible. Just the thought of Gina's devastated expression made her shake all over again. She was going to find Park, and when she did, the next notice the paper ran about him would be his obituary.

"Excuse me, miss, but—"

Tess ignored the receptionist and stomped through the doors into the law offices themselves.

Several startled secretaries looked up, and one, a medium-size guy with glasses, actually tried to head her off, but when Park emerged unknowing from his office, she bore down on him with a murderous single-mindedness that quelled everything in her path.

She grabbed Park's lapel as he spoke to his secretary and pulled him around, his startled face only inches from hers. "I want to see you *now*, you rotten bastard," she hissed. "You want this in public or in private?"

"I, uh, have a client in my office . . ." Park began, babbling in shock.

"Here." A calm brunette in her thirties opened an office door across the way. "Use Nick's office."

"I don't think so, Christine—" Park said, but Tess said, "Great," and when Park said, "Really, I can't—" she grabbed his tie and yanked him across the floor into the office, slamming the door behind them.

"You rotten, lousy, lying scum of a cheating creep," Tess spat at him, backing him up against the wall. "You had to hurt her, didn't you? It was too much trouble to break it off, too tough for you to tell her you couldn't see her anymore, so you just let it go on and on and on and then you let her find out from a damn *newspaper* article!"

"What are you talking about?" Park asked.

That stopped her. Park looked terrified, but he also looked clueless. There was no guilt on his face at all. God, he was dumb. He didn't even realize what he'd done to Gina with that announcement. "Gina," she spat at him. "I'm talking about what you did to Gina."

Park grabbed her shoulders. "What happened to Gina? Is she hurt? What—"

"Of course, she's hurt, you jackass," Tess said, shrugging out of his grip. "She just read about your engagement in the paper. She thought you loved her, she really thought—"

"What engagement?" Park said. "I'm not engaged. Gina thinks I'm engaged?"

"The paper says you're engaged," Tess said, but her voice went down an octave as she frowned at him. "To Corinne."

The expression on Park's face took away the last of her rage. Obviously if there was one thing Park didn't want, it was to be engaged to Corinne.

"Park," Tess said calmly, "somebody told the paper you were marrying Corinne. Was that a mistake?"

"Oh, God," Park said. "And Gina read that? I've got to talk to her." He lunged past Tess for Nick's phone, and Tess followed him, relieved but perplexed.

"Who would tell the paper you were engaged?" she asked him as he punched numbers on the phone like a madman. "And why would the paper believe him? Or her? Corinne? Would Corinne do it?"

"No," Park said grimly, and then his expression changed. "Gina? Gina? No, wait, Gina—" He put the phone down and swallowed hard as he looked at Tess. "She hung up as soon as she heard my voice."

"She's really devastated, Park."

"I didn't do it," he said plaintively. "I wouldn't do that to her. I didn't do it."

"I know," Tess said. "I realize that. It's the only reason you're still living. Sit down."

Park sank into Nick's office chair and buried his face in his hands. "My father did this," he said through his fingers. "He wants me to get married and he picked out Corinne and now he's forcing my hand."

"He really thought if he just announced you were marrying her, you'd do it?" Tess asked incredulously.

Park looked up from his hands. "I probably would have if I hadn't met Gina. I've had a lot of Corinnes in my life. Might as well marry one."

Tess sat down across from him. "You're going to marry Corinne? You can't be serious. What about Gina?"

Park put his head back in his hands again. "She won't talk to me."

Tess resisted the urge to slap him. "Park, explain something to me. What the hell have you been doing with Gina and Corinne in the past month?"

Park leaned back and closed his eyes in pain. "I meant to tell Gina I couldn't see her anymore. I knew my dad wouldn't like her, and there was Corinne. I meant to leave Gina. But I couldn't." He opened his eyes and looked at Tess in abject misery. "I just couldn't." He swallowed. "I made up my mind to do it after Nick pointed out yesterday what a mess I was making. I went over there last night, and I was going to do it. I really was."

He stopped, and Tess watched him, ready to disbelieve everything he said but feeling sorry for him at the same time in spite of herself.

"And she opened the door," Park said finally, "and she was just . . . *beaming* at me, and I thought she'd won the lottery or something, her smile was that big. I asked what happened, and she said . . ." Park swallowed again. "She said, 'You're here.'" He blinked at Tess. "'You're here.' That's all it was. That big goofy smile just because I was there. Nobody ever smiled like that at me before."

Tess leaned back in her own chair, newly sympathetic, but still fed up with how self-centered he was. "And that's when you knew you couldn't leave her—when you realized she loved you," she said derisively. "Well, terrific, Park, but that still leaves Gina out in the cold."

"No," Park said. "That's when I knew I loved her."

Tess eyed him skeptically. "Because she gets a big goofy smile every time she sees you?"

"No," Park said. "Because I get the same big goofy smile every time I see her."

Park's face creased into a big goofy smile at the thought, and Tess closed her eyes and groaned. "Don't do this to me. I was doing much better hating you. Now I have two of you to take care of. Oh, hell."

"What am I going to do?" Park asked. "Gina won't even talk to me."

Tess could hear Nick's voice saying, *Stay out of it.* Well, the hell with him. It was his fault they had two twits for kids. She straightened her shoulders and looked Park in the eye. "All right, here's what you're going to do. First, you're going to call Corinne and tell her you're not engaged. Then you're going to go see Gina and invite her to dinner with us all tonight."

"Dinner with my *father?*" Park said appalled. "He'll be awful to her. I can't do that to her."

"Are you serious about loving her?" Tess demanded.

"Yes, but—"

"Well, she's going to have to meet your parents sooner or later," Tess said. "And under the circumstances, sooner is your best bet. It's only a matter of time before your father gets you engaged to Princess Di."

"He'll be awful to her," Park repeated. "And my mother... Oh, God, my mother—"

"You're just going to have to stand up for her," Tess said. "Gina's going through hell, and she's not going to believe you're serious about her unless you announce it in front of your parents. You owe her."

Park swallowed. "All right." He pulled the phone toward him again and punched a button that connected him to his secretary. "Get me Corinne," he said into the receiver and then looked at Tess.

"Good start," Tess said.

When Park finished breaking off his nonengagement, Tess called Gina.

"Listen to me," she said. "Park is coming over. The engagement was a mistake. He needs to talk to you. Let him in."

"You *made* him do that!" Gina cried hysterically. "I told you not to get involved. You can't make him love me. *Stop it.*"

"Gina, think for a minute. You know how I feel about Park." Tess avoided his eyes as she spoke. "Why would I try to get you two back together if he didn't want that, too? He loves you and he's miserable you got hurt, and he's on his way to your place, so let him in."

"He loves me?" Gina said woefully.

Tess covered the mouthpiece and said, "Go," to Park, who shot out of the office. "He loves you," she said back into the mouthpiece. "Go wash your face and put on some makeup. We're all going to dinner."

TESS STILL HAD half an hour to kill before Nick was due back, and she spent it exploring his office. It was all brown leather and wood, instead of black and white, but it had the same varnished look that everything Nick owned had. The no-body-lives-here look. When she moved around to sit in his desk chair, she saw that even the photograph on his desk was framed in tooled leather.

Her attention caught, Tess took a closer look at the photograph. Whatever she'd expected to find on Nick's desk, it wasn't this.

The picture was the snapshot of them—muddy and disheveled—that she'd had back at her apartment, and she marveled at his keeping it on his desk, since he looked like hell in it. Really attractive hell, but the absolute antithesis of the perfect image he flaunted for his clients. She picked up the picture and stared at it again, remembering how much fun they'd had that day. How much fun they always had. She traced Nick's face with her fingertip, loving him so much she smiled just because his picture was in front of her. If only he was always like that, smiling and relaxed, instead of insatiably chasing that damn partnership. Maybe Nick could change and maybe their kids wouldn't be twits. Park loved Gina. Anything was possible.

She sighed and looked again at herself in the picture. She had a smudge of dirt on her cheek and she looked about ten. That's probably what her kids would look like without Nick's genes to balance hers. She scowled at the picture, cataloging her deficiencies. Her hair was standing straight up and her face was dirty. She was wearing no make up and she was laughing with all her teeth showing.

Tess frowned at the picture, suddenly struck. She did look ten. Ten with crow's feet, but ten just the same.

Or maybe eight.

"Christine?" she called, and Christine appeared in the doorway. "Hi, I'm Tess."

"That was my guess," Christine said. "I'm very pleased to meet you. What did you do to Park?"

"Fixed his life," Tess said. "Tell me, was this picture of me on Nick's desk when Norbert Welch was here?"

"Yes," Christine said.

"Do you think Welch saw it?"

Christine paused for a nanosecond. "He moved around a lot when he was in here. He saw it."

Tess looked at the picture and slowly shook her head. "I'll be damned. I will be damned. I never thought of this." She put the photograph down and asked, "Can I make a long distance call on this phone?"

"Certainly," Christine said. "Press nine to get an outside line."

Five minutes later, Tess had Elise on the line.

"Concentrate darling," she told her mother. "This is important. Remember when I asked you about Lanny?"

"Of course I remember," Elise said. "I'm not senile."

"Right. I'm sorry." Tess tried again. "Somebody else was looking for that manuscript and he found it. What I couldn't figure out was *how* he found it. But then I thought, what if this guy knew Lanny, too? What if he was in the commune with us when Lanny wrote the story? So I want you to remember if there was another guy around that summer. Shorter than Lanny. Fatter. Maybe a little older."

"Well, there were a lot of men in the commune, dear."

"This one's name was Welch," Tess said. "Norbert Welch."

"No," Elise said slowly. "I don't remember anyone by that name."

"Damn," Tess said. "I was sure this guy had recognized my picture and that's why he invited me to his party—to see if I'd remember the story. It was too big of a coincidence otherwise. The commune and me and Lanny and the story... How could Welch have—"

"The only Welch I remember was Lanny," Elise said.

Tess dropped the photo. *"What?"*

"Lanny Welch," Elise said. "He was the only one. No Norbert."

"Lanny's name was Welch? Why didn't you tell me?"

"You didn't ask. And I didn't remember it until you said the name. We didn't use last names much. Is it important?"

"Yes. Thanks, Elise." Tess hung up in a daze. Lanny Welch? A brother of Norbert's maybe? But then why had Norbert recognized her picture if he wasn't at the commune? She punched a button on the intercom. "Christine? Is Norbert Welch's real name Norbert Welch?"

"Yes," Christine said. "Norbert Nolan Welch."

Tess blinked. "Nolan?"

"Nick just called," Christine said. "He's on his way in. He said to tell you he's sorry you had to wait and he hopes you're not bored."

"No," Tess said, trying to digest what she'd just learned. "I'm not bored."

Nolan.

Lanny.

Norbert Welch was Lanny.

The office swung around and then righted itself as she tried to decide how she felt about that, about how Lanny's greatest enemy was Lanny himself, about how Lanny had betrayed everything he believed in and everything she believed in, too, about how her quest to save a long-lost friend ended in losing that friend forever. Lanny wasn't dead, but he might as well have been.

He was Welch.

But somehow, once she'd absorbed the enormity of the fact, that wasn't where her mind wanted to go. It wanted to think about Nick. Nick and that partnership. No matter how she felt about that damn partnership, it was vital to Nick and it rested on Welch. And now she had Welch right where she wanted him. Welch wanted to run for office as a conservative, but she could tell the world he'd been a radical in the sixties, that he'd written the fairy tale he was making fun of and had meant every word of it at the time. His snotty little book wouldn't seem nearly as funny if people knew he'd written the fairy tale in the first place. It didn't seem like much to her, but it would to Welch because it would make him look foolish. All she had to do was say, "Don't publish that book or I'll tell the world about Lanny and CinderTess," and she had him. Everything was in place, and the book wouldn't be published.

And Nick wouldn't get the account, because without the book there was no contract to negotiate.

She looked at it from every angle she could for the next fifteen minutes, and from every angle it looked the same. If she stopped the book, she stopped the partnership. If she didn't stop the book, she was sacrificing everything she believed in for Nick's partnership.

Hello, Mrs. Jekyll.

"Oh, damn," she said, and Nick heard her as he breezed through the door.

"What's up?" he said, dropping his briefcase on the desk. "No, don't tell me now. We've got five minutes before we have to be at the restaurant. What the hell are you wearing?"

Tess looked down at her T-shirt and miniskirt, momentarily distracted. "I just grabbed something," she said. "Gina—"

"Oh, great," he said. "And we're having dinner at The Levee. *Christine!*"

The secretary appeared in the doorway. "You bellowed?"

"Did you replace that jacket?" Nick said, not taking his eyes off Tess. "If you cover up that god-awful T-shirt, the skirt won't look too bad. Good thing you've got great legs."

Christine faded out of the room and then back in, handing Nick a suit box. "Donna Karen, navy pinstripe," she said. "Don't say I didn't warn you."

Tess froze, looking at the box.

"Warn me about what?" Nick said, but Christine was already gone.

"What's in that box?" Tess asked in a strangled voice.

Nick handed it to her. "A suit jacket. You'll look great. Put it on and let's go."

"I have a suit jacket. A great navy jacket. I love that jacket."

"This one is better." Nick snapped his fingers at her and moved back toward the door. "Move it, babe."

"No," Tess said, and Nick froze at the edge in her voice and then turned to face her. "You took my jacket," she said coldly. "I told you not to, and you took my jacket."

"Tess, it was moth-eaten and it looked like hell," Nick said. "What's the big deal?"

"The big deal is that it was my jacket, and you didn't like it so you threw it out. And you're doing the same thing to me." Tess thrust out her chin. "You're throwing me out. You're turning me into Mrs. Jekyll. Be quiet, be polite, don't get involved. I listened to you and almost let Park and Gina screw up their lives. I know you want me to stay out of things and just look decorative, but I can't, Nick. I can't live in designer clothes with my hands tied behind my back while everything goes wrong around me. Today I had to explain to Gina why I stood by and let Park lie to her, and somehow 'Nick asked me not to get involved' didn't quite satisfy either one of us."

"She found out?" Nick said, appalled.

"Park's dad told the society page his son was marrying Corinne."

"Oh, hell." Nick closed his eyes and tipped his head back a little before he looked at her again. "So now what?"

"I fixed it," Tess said. "Park's introducing Gina to his parents tonight at dinner."

Nick looked at her as if she were insane. "Oh, great, you fixed it all right. That's great. That'll impress Welch."

"Welch has his own problem," Tess said. "Me."

Nick stopped, wary. "Tess, I told you if you waited unt after dinner—"

"You're always telling me," Tess said. "Now I'm telling yo There are things that are wrong in my life. And I'm going fix them. And if you can't deal with that, then you can't de with me. You've got to take me as I am, or not take me at all.

"Is that an ultimatum?" Nick asked, his jaw tight.

"Pretty much," Tess said. "I tried it your way. I can't do i So this is it." She swallowed once, and when Nick didn't sa anything, she put the suit box down on the desk and opene it. The jacket was beautiful. She took it out and shook it on but then was distracted by something else in the box. Sh dropped the new jacket on the desk and pulled back the ti: sue paper. "Well, good for Christine," she said, and pulled he old jacket from the box. She shrugged into it not looking Nick. "We'd better get a move on. We're going to be late f dinner," she said, and then she looked at him, defiant in he tattered tweed.

Nick opened the door, stone-faced, and followed her ou

12

THEY WERE LATE to the restaurant, and Kent and Melisande and Welch were already seated. Tess could see them through the archway, a little triumvirate of privilege and arrogance, and she thought about how rude she wanted to be and how ineffectual rudeness would be. Nick had taught her something. Tact. Diplomacy. Underhandedness. She was going to charm the socks right off Welch and then attack him when he was well fed—just like taking a pig to the slaughter.

"If I'm going to behave all night, I need a drink," Tess said.

"Get me one, too," Park said behind them, and Tess turned to see Gina standing blankly beside him, her eyes red from crying, her face slack with fear.

"Gina?" she said. "Are you all right?"

"I'm fine," Gina said. "I'm perfectly fine. Everything's going to be fine. I'm ready to meet Park's parents. Really I am. I'm fine."

"I'm not," Park said. "Get me a drink. We took a cab, so drunkenness is not a problem."

"Gina, honey?" Tess asked.

"I'm fine," Gina said again. "Can I have some gum?"

"No," Tess said.

"Oh, hell," Nick said.

THE SEATING ARRANGEMENTS could have been better, Nick thought as he surveyed the situation. Somehow they'd ended up with the Pattersons on one side of the big round table, staring across at Park and Gina who had Welch on one side and him and Tess on the other. Park winced under his fa-

ther's gaze like a sinner on Judgment Day with a few thing
to explain about the little ethnic woman by his side who wa
obviously not Radcliffe material, while Gina sat, dazed wit
terror, across from Melisande, a woman who was neve
amused and often appalled. And clearly, Melisande had neve
had as much to be appalled about as she had now. In des
peration Nick gestured to the waiter.

"Bring wine," Nick told him. "Any wine. Now."

"Very good, sir," the waiter said.

Kent Patterson smiled tightly. "The Chateau Rothschild
Dennis."

"Very good, sir."

Kent Patterson commandeered the menu. "I'll order for u
all." He didn't see Welch roll his eyes as he began. "We'll sta
with the gravlax and pumpkin soup," he said, relaxing as h
exerted authority. "And then the goat cheese and endive. It'
very good. Remarkable, really. Then the Muscovy duck, an
for dessert crème brûlée."

"*Very* good, sir," Dennis said to Kent.

"Steak," Welch said. "Rare. Baked potato. And a blood
Mary."

"Henderson is not going to be pleased," Tess said to him

"Henderson is not going to know," Welch said to he
"Unless you rat on me."

"I should for your own good," Tess said. "Somebod
should tell the truth and save you from yourself."

Welch looked startled by her tone, but then Kent spoke t
him and he looked away.

"What's going on?" Nick whispered to her as Dennis a
rived with the wine.

"The dinner party from hell," Tess said. "You may want t
leave now. It's going to get ugly."

Then Kent turned away from Welch and caught sight of hi
quivering son. He picked up his glass in disgust and drank hi
wine.

Melisande looked down her long nose at Gina without blinking and drank her wine.

Gina shook visibly and drank her wine.

Park sighed and drank his wine.

Tess looked at Nick, and they both drank their wine.

"So Park tells me you're a Democrat," Kent said to Tess. "That must make for some interesting conversations with Nick."

"Oh, a few," Tess said.

"Democrats," Welch snorted, but he watched Tess with the same rapt attention he always gave her, only this time a little more warily than usual.

Kent smiled at Tess patronizingly. "So is it true that politics make strange bedfellows?"

"Really, Kent," Melisande said with cold distaste.

"Bedpersons," Park said, and everybody stared at him.

"What?" Kent asked.

"Bedpersons," Park said again. "Tess would prefer bedpersons. It's nongender-specific."

"Don't be an idiot," Kent said, and Park flushed.

"He's not," Tess said, struck by Park's thoughtfulness if not by his brains. "He's right. I prefer bedpersons," she lied.

"Politically correct garbage," Welch said, but he sounded distracted.

"Not much conviction there," Tess said. "Changing your mind? *Again?*"

"What?" Welch said, and now the wariness was palpable.

"Bedpersons? How odd," Melisande said, and then she stared at Gina as if she was the offender.

"I think I'd prefer another drink," Nick said, ignoring the bottle on the table in an attempt to distract Melisande. "Waiter?"

Another waiter brought more wine and genuflected, while Dennis presided over the distribution of the gravlax, be-

stowing it as if it were the loaves and fishes, instead of jus
the fishes.

Tess looked down at her plate. "What is this stuff, any
way? From the name, I thought it was going to be fill dirt."

"Pickled salmon," Nick said.

Tess looked at the oily pink slab in disgust. "If I ever go ou
to eat with you again," she said, "we're going to Burger King."

"Tell me about yourself, Miss DaCosta," Melisande said
to Gina when the salmon had been replaced by the pumpkin
soup. She'd waited until Gina was sipping soup to ask, and
Gina was so startled that she dropped her spoon in her bow
and splattered the peach tablecloth.

"Oh, I'm sorry, I'm sorry." Gina grabbed her napkin to
mop up, and Park trapped her fingers with his hand and
smiled at her.

"Gina is very talented," Tess said. "She has a wonderfu
singing voice."

"Opera?" Melisande inquired smoothly.

"No," Park said. "Musical comedy."

Gina smiled at him wanly.

Nick picked up the bread plate and shoved it under Meli
sande's nose. "More bread?"

"No," she said shortly, and turned back to Gina. "So where
did you go to school? Perhaps we're alumnae together."

"Brush High School," Gina said miserably. "It's in Euclid
In Cleveland."

"No, no, dear, I meant college," Melisande said.

"Try the pumpkin soup, Mrs. Patterson," Tess said. "It'
very thick."

"I didn't go to college," Gina said. "I didn't even graduat
from high school. I went on the road with a touring com
pany of *Oklahoma!* when I was sixteen, and that's what I've
been doing for the past eighteen years."

"So, you're a chorus girl," Melisande said, pleased to have
made her point.

"Yes," Gina said, and drank all the wine in her glass.

Park began to turn an odd shade of pink under his tan. "Mother, I don't think—"

"Did I tell you I saw Susan Vandervalk on the Cape, Park?" Melisande said. "She always asks after you. She's just finished her master's, and now she's volunteering at the art museum. A lovely girl. You should call her. Remember how much fun you had with her that summer in Paris?"

"No," Park said, and Melisande blinked at the word, while Welch choked on his bloody Mary and then grinned at Park in appreciation.

Tess knocked her fork on the floor and pulled Nick's sleeve as she bent down to retrieve it.

"What?" he said when they were both below table level. He sounded both distracted and annoyed.

"You might want to announce publicly that we're splitting up now, because I'm going to kill her before dessert and that way you won't be involved," Tess said, and Nick flinched at the words "splitting up."

"Wait a minute," he said.

Tess shook her head. "I know it's not an adult thing to do, but that hag has it coming."

"I agree," Nick said. "But get a grip. You'll just embarrass Gina more if you say something. This can't go on forever. I think Gina and Park have the right idea. Keep drinking."

"There's not enough alcohol in the world," Tess said.

"And we're not splitting up," Nick went on. "I hate that damn jacket, but we're not splitting up over it. You can wear sackcloth and ashes if you want, but we're staying together."

"It's not just the jacket. There's more."

Then they heard Melisande saying, "Really, children, the waiter will take care of the fork."

They both swiveled their heads to see the waiter looking down at them.

"The waiter will take care of the fork, Tess," Nick said, and crossed his eyes at her.

"Of course, how provincial of me," Tess said, and they both straightened in their chairs.

"More wine, please," Nick said to the waiter. "Keep it coming."

By the time the soup was removed, they were all sitting in an alcoholic haze that somehow was not enough to cut the tension. A machete wouldn't have cut the tension, Tess decided. Maybe a chain saw. Maybe if Dennis showed up in a hockey mask and . . .

Dennis showed up with the goat cheese.

"Ah, goat cheese," Kent said when the salad plate was placed before him.

"Goat cheese," Tess said, focusing on it through her wine fog. "I hate this stuff. We used to live in a commune, and I had to milk the goats so we could make this. You wouldn't believe—"

Nick kicked her smartly on the ankle, and she realized she was blithering and shut up before she remembered that she was going to blither from now on whenever she felt like it. She opened her mouth to ask Welch if he remembered the goat cheese, but stopped when Melisande Patterson interrupted her.

"Goats?" Melisande looked at Tess with such tipsy horror that Tess wondered if this was the first time Melisande had realized that goat cheese didn't just spring miraculously from the endive nestled next to it. "You had goats?"

"Of course, goats, Melisande," Kent said in exasperation.

Melisande turned snapping black eyes on him, and Nick preempted her swiftly. "So, Kent, what's new on the coast?"

"How amusing you should ask," Melisande said, preempting in return. "We just had a lovely dinner with the Whitneys. Do you remember the Whitneys, Nick? You and

Park dated their daughters in college. Bea and Bunny. Remember?"

"Vividly," Nick said while Tess choked on her drink.

Melisande purred her approval. "Park was quite serious about Bunny. She asked after you at dinner, Park. She's still quite lovely. You should call her."

"No," Park said flatly over his wineglass, and Melisande flinched.

"You know, I'm really enjoying this dinner," Welch said.

"Wait a minute, is that true?" Tess said to Nick when she'd wiped her mouth. "They were actually called Bea and Bunny?"

"You find that amusing, Miss Newhart?" Melisande's voice was cold.

"I find that hysterical," Tess said.

"I don't get it," Gina said, peering at them as she lifted her wineglass.

"I believe Miss DaCosta has had enough wine," Melisande said.

Gina blinked at her.

"Perhaps you're not used to drinking wine, dear," Melisande went on. "I'm sure Dennis could find you something you'd prefer. Perhaps a beer?"

Park's flushed tan deepened to puce. "That's enough, Mother."

Gina drained her glass.

"She's *Italian*," Tess said to Melisande. "They *invented* wine. And they never named anybody Bunny and BeeBee."

"Bunny and Bea," Melisande corrected, her head only wobbling slightly from the wine.

"You think that's an improvement?" Tess said.

"This is excellent goat cheese," Nick said.

"More wine, please," Gina said in desperation.

"How Italian of you, dear," Melisande said.

"*Mother*," Park said disgustedly.

"Listen, you—" Tess began, and then Nick knocked his fork off the table and pulled her down below the edge with him.

"Don't do it," he whispered to her. "I know she's a horror, but don't do it."

"How come she's the only one who gets to be rude?" Tess asked. "The hell with this civilization garbage. I'm taking her on."

"No," Nick said, and then Melisande said, "Children, the waiter will get the fork."

"Thank God, you're an orphan," Tess said.

"If Salvador Dali gave a dinner party, it would look just like this one," Nick whispered back. "Thank God we're drunk or we'd have to kill ourselves. Listen, I love you."

"What?" Tess said.

"I love you," Nick said. "I don't know what's going on here, but I love you. I know you're up to something, and I don't give a damn. I love you."

"Tell me our kids don't have to take swimming lessons," Tess said.

Nick was puzzled. "You want them to drown?"

"Children," Melisande began again, and Tess pulled herself back upright, using the table edge for leverage.

"Look," she said. "We're conferring down here. The fork bit is just a subterfuge, okay? It's a ruse. Deal with it."

Then she ducked down next to Nick.

"Very smooth," he said. "I think we're off their Christmas-card list now."

"Oh, damn," Tess said, and they both burst out laughing. Then Tess remembered Welch and stopped. "It's not funny. This is terrible."

"What?" Nick said.

"Children!" Melisande said, and they sat up again, both confused and one miserable.

The duck medallions arrived accompanied by three green beans, two carrot slivers and a perfect new potato. Welch looked at the other plates, snorted and cut into his steak.

"Do you suppose Dennis has been snacking from the plates?" Tess asked Nick. "I seem to be missing some veggies."

"This is it," Nick said. "This is haute cuisine. Try not to roll in it."

"I hate this life," Tess said.

Nick frowned, confused. "Because of the vegetables?"

"No," Tess said. "I miss color. I hate all that black and white. And I hate those damn new clothes. And I hate this stupid restaurant."

Nick put down his fork. "Okay," he said, slowly. "What do you like?"

"You," Tess said. "I love you. And I'm going to destroy your life."

Nick blinked. "Not unless you leave me."

Tess dropped her fork and pulled him below the table again. "I can stop the book," she said to Nick and watched while he closed his eyes.

"Tell me," he said, his eyes still closed.

"Welch is Lanny," Tess said. "He wrote the fairy tale to begin with. He protested the war. He's making fun of himself."

Nick opened his eyes. "That might not stop the book."

Tess nodded. "Yes, it will. Think of his pride."

Nick set his jaw. "I'm too confused to think this through right now. Let's just cut to the chase here. Is there anything I can say that will make you stop this? I know this is important to you, I do understand that, but this is my partnership. I need it, Tess."

Tess looked at him and saw the need in his eyes, but she also saw the strength and generosity there. He'd saved Angela, got the locks put on the doors, fixed Gina up with a job, helped Tess get a chance at Decker and loved her into physical and emotional ecstasy, and now she was going to destroy his hopes. And . . . and in the process she'd lose him. She'd be without him forever! Suddenly, she felt dizzy and it wasn't from the wine. The thought of life without Nick was too cold and immense to absorb without reeling. "You can stop me," she whispered.

"Great," he said, visibly relieved. "What do I have to do?"

"Tell me you'll leave me," Tess said, and Nick's jaw dropped. "This is important to me," she went on. "But I don't ever want to spend another day away from you. I love you. If you tell me this will break us up, I won't do it."

Nick cupped her cheek with his hand. "I'd never say that. I would never do that. I love you. The partnership's important, but I would never—"

"You don't know that," Tess said, suddenly sure of what she was doing. "You'd resent it, after all that work you've put into this. It could finish us."

"No," Nick began again, and then Melisande said *"Children."*

"I won't do it," Tess said, and straightened back in her chair.

"You are being excessively rude," Melisande said when Nick had straightened, also, but Nick ignored her and faced Welch.

"So Tess tells me you're Lanny," he said to the older man. "Big switch on that fairy tale you wrote. How do you plan to explain that, anyway?"

Welch jerked his head up sharply and then looked at Tess.

But Tess was staring at Nick. "Are you crazy?"

"Evidently." Nick slumped back in his chair. "But now I've got nobody to resent but myself."

"God, I love you," Tess said.

"What's this all about?" Kent said, confused and not pleased about it.

Tess turned back to Welch. "How have you been, Lanny?" she asked softly.

Welch relaxed suddenly, and looked so relieved that Tess wondered if he was glad he'd been found out. "I didn't think you'd ever catch on," he said to her. "You used to be a lot sharper."

"You used to be a lot taller," Tess shot back.

Welch snorted. "You used to be a lot shorter."

"And your hair was brown and you weren't this fat," Tess finished.

"Really, Tess," Kent said. "That's hardly—"

"I'm not fat," Welch interrupted him.

"Yes, you are," Tess said. "You've changed. Imagine how many people will find that interesting."

"Not that many," Welch said.

"Care to risk it?" Tess said. "Should make for some interesting stories during your campaign."

"I don't have to risk it. I've got a new job," Welch announced, and Tess blinked at the sudden swerve in the conversation. "I'm on the board of the Decker Academy. Heard of it?"

Tess was knocked speechless.

"Thought you had," Welch said smugly. "Understand we're voting on the teaching contracts tomorrow. Only takes one no vote to stop a hire."

"Well, you are a son of a bitch," Tess said in equal parts resignation and admiration.

"*Tess*," Kent said. "Nick, really—"

"Checkmate," Welch said. "Knew as soon as you said Decker at that dinner party that I had you." He settled back in his chair.

Tess folded her arms. "I withdraw my application. The hell with you."

Welch met her eyes and then nodded. "I figured that's what you'd do." He shrugged. "So, go ahead," he said. "Do it."

"You know, I loved you," Tess told him, and Kent's eyes popped out of his head. "You meant everything to me. You taught me everything. You taught me who I was."

Welch shook his head. "No, I didn't. You always knew who you were. I just gave you a boot in the rear when you needed it."

"When you wrote that damn book, I thought you'd ruined everything," Tess said. "I'm still mad about it. I still hate that you did it."

"Yeah, I was afraid of that," Welch said. "Damn near had a heart attack when I saw your picture in the paper with Jamieson here at the opera. And then that picture in his office." He laughed. "It was like seeing a ghost. My past coming back to haunt me. Tessie Newhart."

"I wondered about that," Tess said. "It seemed too big of a coincidence for you to just happen to invite me to that reading. So you saw the picture and then went after Nick to get me." She considered it and then nodded. "Not bad. Very Lanny-like." She tilted her head at him. "I liked you again, you know. Even these past weeks when I was mad as hell at you, I liked you. Lanny's still in you somewhere."

"The hell he is," Welch said. "So come on, kid, let's get this over with. Make your move."

Tess turned to Nick, and Nick shrugged. "Do it," he said. "You will, anyway."

"What the hell is going on?" Kent asked.

Tess looked across at Welch, searching for Lanny and not finding him. Welch was right. He was gone, the past was gone, and all she had was now. Now and Nick. But she also had all the lessons that Lanny had taught her—including the one about not fighting unless you cared enough about the cause and could stand to lose what you were going to lose.

"Nothing's going on," Tess said. "Absolutely nothing."

"Chicken," Welch said.

"Nope," Tess said. "There are some causes worth sacrific-
ng people for. This isn't one of them. You just be damn
rateful you've got the best lawyer in town working for you."

"Why, thank you, Tess," Kent said, thawing toward her.

"Not you. I meant Nick," Tess said.

"Well, really, Tess," Kent said, freezing again. "I'm Nor-
ert's lawyer."

"No, you're not. You're fired," Welch said to him.

"*What?*" Tess said. "After I just—"

"This is her fault," Kent said to Nick, jabbing a finger at
ess. "She's completely unsuitable and you know it. What
ou—"

"Tess and I are getting married," Nick said evenly. "Be very
areful what you say about her."

"Oh, really, Nick," Melisande said, the alcohol making her
ud. "This is the outside of enough. Don't make foolish of-
rs. The woman might actually hold you to it." She waved
er hand in front of her. "And then you'll be vulnerable to a
reach-of-promise suit."

"He's serious, Mother," Park said. "And so am I." He took
deep breath. "I'm going to marry Gina—if she'll have me."
Gina made a small sound next to him and clutched the
ble.

"Oh, well, that's just fine," Kent said, sounding like a
hiny two-year-old. "Just fine."

"*You are not marrying that tramp,*" Melisande spat at her
n, the venom in her voice freezing everyone except Tess,
ho slapped the table and made the flatware jump.

"Listen, lady," she said to Melisande. "I'm having a tense
ening here, and I'm not fooling around. You take one more
ot at my friend, and there will be consequences."

"Mother, stop it," Park said. "I mean it, stop it *now*."

Melisande rested her chin on her swaying hand and stared
Park, her head bobbing and weaving like a cobra. "The
st nannies. The best schools. The best colleges."

"Three of them before I was a sophomore," Park said. "Didn't it ever occur to you that maybe—"

Melisande straightened suddenly and pointed one beautifully manicured claw at Park. "You are *not* marrying a cheap Italian tramp, and that's final."

"Oh, no," Gina moaned faintly.

Park threw down his napkin and looked at his mother levelly. "I am marrying Gina. If you make me choose between you, I am choosing Gina. And if you ever say another insulting word to her, if you ever address her with anything but absolute respect, I'm never speaking to you again."

Melisande's mouth dropped open.

"I mean it," Park said. "Don't push me on this. I love her and I'm marrying her, and that's it."

"Don't be ridiculous," Kent began. "You can't—"

"And that goes double for you," Park said to him.

Kent turned purple with indignation.

"Good for you, kid," Welch said. "I didn't know you had it in you."

"Then you're no son of mine," Kent said. "I disown you, you ungrateful whelp." He turned his glare on Nick. "And you're fired. In fact, you're both fired."

"*Oh, God,*" Gina said.

Then she put her head under the table and threw up.

The rest of the table froze, and even Dennis suddenly seemed at a loss.

"Uh, waiter?" Nick called. "It's not a fork this time."

"Shut up," Tess said, trying to peer under the table to see if Gina was all right.

"Well, they were a hell of a lot faster when it was forks," Nick said.

"Gina? Honey?" Park had put his head under the table, too.

Welch dipped his napkin in the glass and bent under the table to give it to Gina. "Don't worry, kid," they heard him

y. "It's that rich crap they serve here. Smartest thing you
an do is get rid of it."

"My shoes," Melisande said in shock. "They're Manolo
ahnik, and she . . . she . . ."

"I told you there'd be consequences," Tess said.

CK HUSTLED the four of them out the door and into a taxi
efore any blood could be spilled.

"I can't believe it," Gina said when Park had pulled her
ato his lap to make room for Tess and Nick in the back of
e cab. "I just can't believe it. I barfed at The Levee on your
other's shoes. Oh, God, I want to die."

Tess patted her hand, and Nick gave the cabby Park's
ddress.

"I've ruined your life," Gina said to Park as the cab pulled
vay. Her head dropped drunkenly on his shoulder. "I've
uined your life forever."

Park considered it. "How?"

"I embarrassed you in that restaurant," Gina moaned.

"Actually right up until the time you returned your din-
r, you were the quietest of all of us," Nick said. "You're
obably the only one of us who *wasn't* embarrassing."

"They'll never let you in there again," Gina sobbed.

"At those prices, who cares?" Tess said.

"And your parents will never speak to you again," Gina
ailed.

"Get her the biggest diamond in Riverbend," Tess told
rk. "There's no way you can repay her for that, but at least
u can show your appreciation."

"It's not funny," Gina said. "It's awful."

"It's not that awful," Park said. "They never liked me
uch, anyway. And let's face it, I'm the only son they have.
ey'll have to take me back. It's not like they have a choice."

"They don't deserve you," Gina said.

"Oh, I don't know—" Park began.

"No," Tess said. "She's right. They don't. And I owe yo‹
an apology, too. I'm sorry I've been so nasty. Although yo‹
deserve some of it for two-timing Gina, you creep."

"He's not a creep," Gina said, leaning on him drunkenl‹
"He's the most wonderful, thoughtful, darling, disinherit‹
man on the planet, and I love him." She looked up at him ‹
the dim light of the cab. "And I threw up on his mothe‹
shoes," she wailed. Her head dropped like a stone on ‹
shoulder.

"You know, she's not a good drunk," Nick said after so‹
thought. Tess glared at him and he shrugged. "Just ‹
observation."

"I think she's perfect," Park said. "I don't deserve her."

"Oh, no, you do, you do." Gina raised her head and star‹
into Park's eyes. "But I don't deserve *you*."

"I'm going to lose *my* Muscovy duck if this doesn't light‹
up pretty soon," Tess said. "For heaven's sake, Gina, all yo‹
did was blow dinner. It's not like anybody died. Get over i‹

Gina groaned and let her head plummet back onto Par‹
shoulder.

"Gina? Honey?" Park said, concerned, and Gina wav‹
her hand, barely conscious as the cab slowed to a stop in fr‹
of Park's apartment building. "We're going to go now,"‹
said to Nick. "God, this was a terrible evening."

"I know," Nick said in comfort. "But it's over. And no‹
of those disgusting people are talking to us anymore, so w‹
never have to do it again."

"Good point," Park said. He got out of the cab and th‹
helped Gina out. "You okay?" he asked her.

"No," Tess answered before Gina could. "I'm very co‹
fused."

"She's my problem," Nick said to Park. "Take yours ‹
stairs and get some coffee into her."

"Let's all have breakfast tomorrow before you go to work," ess said. "Pancakes. That would be nice. That might cheer e up. With pecans."

Gina moaned.

"What work?" Nick said. "We just got fired."

"Right. I forgot. Sorry," Tess said. "That was insensitive f me."

Park sighed. "Why not. Tomorrow at eight. Breakfast at e River Inn, and then we can go clear out our desks."

"You know," Nick said to Park, "we're not completely rewed here. We could go into partnership ourselves. Hell, e did all the work, anyway."

Park nodded. "I've thought of that before—"

"The River Inn. Don't you ever go anyplace that isn't pre-ntious and overpriced?" Tess asked.

"No," Park said sadly. "I'm a product of my upbringing."

"Oh." Tess winced. "Sorry. I'm being insensitive again. It's cause I'm drunk."

"That's all right," Park said. "I'm drunk, too, so it doesn't rt." He bent to kiss Tess's cheek, and Gina swayed dan-rously against him as he moved. "Steady, love," he said to ina as he tightened his hold on her.

"You're a nice person, Park," Tess said. "I forgive you the ss Trueheart bit."

"Thank you," Park said. "I forgive you the low-income-using crack."

"I liked you both better when you were fighting," Nick d. "This is kind of sickening, and I was nauseated to begin th."

When the cab was moving again, Tess put her head on ck's shoulder. "You know, now that you're out of work, I uld start looking for another place. You can't afford to ep me any longer, and I'm not going to be working at cker, that's for damn sure."

"Okay," Nick said. "Let's get married while you're look
ing."

Tess lifted her head from his shoulder. "Marriage? I can't
I love you, but I just can't."

"Why not? If this is guilt over sabotaging my career, los
it. The more I think about it, the more I think I had a caree
that needed to be sabotaged. The thought of not working fc
Kent Patterson anymore is strangely cheering."

"That's not it," she said. "It's selfish. If I marry you, I en
up living in the Crystal Palace and wearing somebody else
clothes." She shook her head. "It's nothing personal. I lov
you. I tried to sacrifice for your career. I just can't stand you
life."

"I know," Nick said. "You keep telling me. I can adapt. Yo
can keep your clothes. We can paint the house red. Wha
ever it takes to get you."

"You don't have to adapt. I'm just afraid to get married. Yo
can still have me." Tess let her head roll back against the sea
"In fact, you've got me."

"No," Nick said. "I want commitment."

"You're drunk. You don't want commitment. You're a gu
Get a grip."

The cab pulled up in front of Nick's house, and he lean
forward to pay the cabbie before he opened the door and g
out. He took Tess's hand to help her out and then he walk
her to the door, his arm tight around her shoulders. "We
talk about it in the morning."

"I didn't do so good, did I?" Tess said, while he unlock
the front door. "Welch is still going to publish that dan
book. And you don't have a job. And neither do I, sin
Welch is going to sink me with Decker." Then she brig
ened. "But on the other hand, I still have my jacket."

"In the morning," Nick repeated, and gave her a gen
shove into the house before following her in.

HE RIVER INN was brimming with hearty, smiling people
vhen the waiter showed Nick to a table the next morning.
Jick peered blearily over the top of his dark glasses, winced,
nd put his glasses back on.

"Coffee," he said to the waiter. "Very, very black."

"Very good, sir," the waiter said.

"Hurry," Nick said, and concentrated on keeping his head
:om exploding while he waited for caffeine and relief.

Park and Gina took chairs across from him just as the
vaiter delivered his cup.

"Why the dark glasses?" Park asked.

"Because I have the hangover from hell, and the sunlight
aakes my brains shudder." Nick picked up his coffee and
pped it carefully.

"Where's Tess?" Gina whipped her head around like a hy-
:eractive bird, bright and tensely eager to enjoy the morn-
ig. Too bright and eager. Her smile looked like it was strung
om her ears.

"Why aren't you in excruciating head-banging pain?" Nick
larled at her.

"Because she threw up again when we got home," Park
aid. "I think she lost everything she'd eaten for the past
onth. Definitely got rid of the alcohol. Nothing left inside
· make her sick. Smart woman. So what about breakfast?"

"Do you mind?" Nick scowled at him. "What did you do—
.row up with her?"

"Me? Oh, I never have hangovers." Park picked up the
enu. "Crepes. How does cherry sauce sound, Gina?"

"Wait a minute." Nick put up his hand. "I'm the healthy
ie around here. I don't drink, smoke, stay up late or run
ound with strange women. So why are you fine and I'm
ing over?"

"Lack of practice," Park said. "You can't just jump into de-
.uchery one night and expect to get the hang of it by morn-
₃. It takes years. And anyway, Tess is strange."

"She is not," Gina said from the depths of the menu.

"Strange in a nice way," Park amended. "But you've got to admit she's different."

"That's true," Gina said. She peered cautiously at Park over the edge of the menu. "How about if I get waffles with blueberry sauce? Then maybe you can have some of mine and I'll take some of your crepes?"

"Great," Park said, and Gina put down the menu and smiled at him shyly.

Nick groaned. "It's too early in the morning for young love. Knock it off."

"Hey, we've been putting up with you and Tess for weeks," Park said. "By the way, where is Tess?"

"Next door at the newsstand, arguing with the clerk." Nick lifted his glasses and tried to find her through the sunlight that screamed through the restaurant. "I don't know what she's doing. I left her because I needed coffee."

"About this new partnership idea—" Park began and then stopped when Tess dropped into the chair beside Nick.

"Mission accomplished," Tess said. "So how are you all this morning? Still engaged?"

Gina stiffened and looked at her with venom iced with despair.

"Of course we're still engaged," Park said. "Why not?"

Gina's mouth fell open and she turned to face him. "You mean it?"

He looked at her in surprise. "Of course I mean it. Why would I change my mind?"

Gina blinked and swallowed. "Well, you were drunk when you asked me. And then I threw up in the most expensive restaurant in town in front of your parents and half of Riverbend society. And—"

"I'm sober now," Park said. "Will you marry me?"

"Yes," Gina said faintly.

"Good," Park said. "Let's order breakfast."

Gina put her hand on his arm. "Don't you care that you'll never be able to go back to The Levee again?"

Park patted her hand. "Gina, The Levee needs us more than we need them. We can go back anytime."

"Us?" Gina said.

"Us," Park said. "Are you going to make me propose again?"

"Probably," Gina said. "I'm having a hard time getting this." She gazed up at him in watery disbelief, and then she began to smile through her tears. "Maybe last night wasn't the worst night of my life."

"Well, personally I enjoyed the evening tremendously," Tess said. "Which is why I just sent a thank-you gift to the Pattersons."

Nick looked at her suspiciously over his sunglasses. "What did you do?"

"I sent them a nice gift subscription," Tess said. "Delivered straight to their door every week." She smiled. "For the next five years."

"A subscription to what?" Nick asked, fairly sure he didn't want to know.

"The *National Enquirer*," Tess said.

"Oh, no," Nick said.

"I thought about the *Sun*," Tess went on, "because it had a lovely cover story about an alien having Elvis's baby in a Stop-and-Go in Minnesota, but I decided that Melisande would rather know that the story about Roseanne Arnold having her thighs sucked is simply a vicious rumor. However, it is true that Liz—"

"You sent my mother a five-year subscription to the *National Enquirer*?" Park said.

"Well, Park, I had to," Tess said. "Any fool knows Elvis was never in Minnesota. And I wanted your mother to have the best."

"Let me buy you breakfast," Park said. "Did you say it's delivered to the door?"

"Every week," Tess said. "And you know, I doubt she'll be able to get it canceled. I understand it's extremely difficult to duck the *National Enquirer*."

"Let me buy you lunch, too."

"MR. PATTERSON asked me to be his secretary," Christine said to Nick when the four of them arrived at the office. "Did you get fired?"

"Did it ever occur to you I might have quit?" Nick asked, exasperated.

"No," Christine said.

Nick gave up. "Yes, I got fired."

"But it was my fault," Tess said.

"So where are we working now?" Christine said to Nick.

Nick blinked. "You're coming with me?"

"It took me a long time to break you in," Christine said. "Also, Mr. Patterson is incompetent." She stared at Park. "Nothing personal."

"It's all right," Park said. "I know he's incompetent. He fired me, too."

Christine remained undisturbed by the news.

"Look, maybe if I talked to him—" Tess began, and both Park and Nick said, *"No!"*

At that moment Kent came out of his office, followed by Welch.

"We're just leaving," Nick said to Kent. "We'll be out as soon as we've—"

"Now, let's not be hasty," Kent said.

"Hasty?" Tess said, outraged, but Nick clamped a hand over her mouth before she could go on.

"Good thinking," Welch said to Nick. "This is why I want you for my lawyer. You scope out the situation and move on it." He turned back to Kent. "I mean it. The only way your firm is handling this book is if Jamieson and your son are in charge. I don't want you anywhere near my account. Got that?"

"Hello?" Nick exchanged a look with Park. Then he smiled genially at Welch. "Well, that would be just fine with me, sir, but we've been fired. Sorry."

"Wait a minute—" Kent began.

Welch grinned at Nick. "Thinking of setting up your own practice?"

"Absolutely," Nick said, and Park nodded.

"Now there's no need for that," Kent said. "I may have let the wine do the talking last night, but I'm a big enough man to realize the error of my ways. You're not fired." He glanced at his son. "Either one of you."

"I'm marrying Gina," Park said. "Get used to it or fire me again."

Kent smiled antiseptically at Gina. "Welcome to the family, my dear," he said with absolutely no enthusiasm.

"Thank you," Gina said, and took Park's hand.

"Well, it's a start," Park said to his father. "Work on your warmth."

"And now Nicholas," Kent said, turning to Nick and Nick said, "No."

"No?" Tess said, but for once Kent was ahead of her.

"What do you want?" he said grimly.

"Partner," Nick said. "I deserve it. Give it to me."

"It's a family firm, son . . ." Kent said.

"Then adopt me," Nick said. "Because I'm walking without it."

"And I'll be with him," Park said. "God knows, I'd never make it without him, anyway."

Welch looked at Tess. "You enjoying this?"

Tess shrugged. "Moderately. I'm still not happy about that damn book."

"It's a good book," Welch said.

"It's a dishonest book," Tess said.

"Young lady, that's no way to talk to your elders," Kent said.

"That's no way to talk to my wife," Nick said at the same time Welch said, "Shut up, Patterson."

Kent glared at Tess but tried to soften the loathing in his voice. "If you're going to marry a member of this firm, my dear, you're going to have to do some growing up."

"No, she doesn't," Nick said. "She stays the way she is. And technically she's not marrying a member of this firm. She's marrying me, and I'm still fired."

"No, you're not." Kent's face creased in pain for a moment and then he said, "I'll get the partnership papers drawn up this afternoon."

"Works for me," Nick said. Then he turned to Tess. "Stop harassing my biggest client."

"Back off, Jamieson," Welch said. "I didn't hire you to protect me from her."

"You'll change your mind," Nick said. "She's stubborn as hell."

"I'm getting married," Gina said suddenly, amazement dawning in her voice.

"I'm not," Tess said.

"Yes, you are," Nick said. "The only person more stubborn than you is me. Besides, I just made partner, so now I can give this marriage thing all my attention."

"Don't bet on it," Tess said.

Welch looked at both of them and laughed.

Tess transferred her attention back to him. "I want to talk to you." She pulled him to one side, away from everyone else.

"If you're going to yell at me about the book, forget it," Welch said. "I like it the way it is."

Tess put her hands on her hips and scowled at him. "That book is crap, Lanny."

Welch closed his eyes and then, after a moment, he opened them and grinned at her. "Twenty-eight years and it seems like yesterday. Damn, I've missed you."

"What?" Tess's surprise made her scowl disappear. "You're not paying attention here. I just insulted you."

"Twenty-eight years ago I was stuck in that commune, trying to figure out why everything suddenly sounded so damn stupid," Welch said to her. "There was Daniel, strutting around like an Old Testament prophet, and he sure as hell sounded like he knew what he was talking about. And Elise." A smile eased onto Welch's face. "Your mother was something else, Tessie. Feminism and free love. Hell of a woman, Elise."

Tess blinked, and Welch returned to earth.

"But I just couldn't buy it anymore," he told her. "All that antiauthority-peace-and-love stuff. It sounded pretty, but I knew it wasn't working, knew it wouldn't work. It was all starting to sound like such garbage, but everybody there believed it, and hell, I was twenty-six. What did I know?"

"You knew everything," Tess said, startled. "I thought you were God."

"And then one day," Welch said, "I was sitting off by myself, trying to figure out why I was so damn uneasy, and you showed up with your hair sticking up and a black eye. You said, 'This turn-the-other-cheek stuff is crap, Lanny,' just like you did now, and I knew you were right. You were the only one in the whole damn place who had a clue."

"And that's when you taught me how to pick my fights," Tess said, remembering. Suddenly there was a lump in her throat. "And then you left me." She was horrified to hear her voice quiver.

Welch looked startled by the emotion in her voice. "I had to," he said. "You showed me the way out."

"I did?" Tess swallowed the lump in her throat. "No. No, you just got bored and left."

"No," Welch said. "I got smart and left. The only thing I regret about leaving is not taking you with me."

"Oh, hell." Tess closed her eyes. "Oh, damn, I wish you had."

Welch snorted. "Yeah. Your mom wouldn't have batted an eye if I'd kidnapped you. Sure."

"She probably wouldn't have noticed," Tess said. "I can't believe you left because of something I said."

"You were a touchstone, Tessie," Welch said. "I always knew whether something was true once I'd floated it by you."

"I was eight," Tess said, dumbfounded.

"Yeah, and you were still smarter than everybody around you," Welch said. "That's why I went after Jamieson. I wanted to hear you laugh at that damn book with me. Validation." He snorted at her in contempt. "I thought you would have caught on by now, but I was wrong. I should never have left you with your parents. They screwed you up good."

"No, they didn't." Tess glared at him and then relented. "Okay, let's try this again. Your book isn't crap. It's just too simplistic."

"I'm not rewriting that book," Welch said. "I'm tired of writing. I'm going into politics."

"Oh, there's a surprise." Tess put her hands on her hips and frowned at him, and he grinned back at her. "Knock it off," she said. "I'm not eight, so stop patronizing me. Here's the deal."

"There is no deal," Welch said.

"You rethink that book and make it balanced—"

"It's satire, damn it. It's not supposed to be balanced," Welch snapped.

"—and I'll campaign for you."

"*What?*"

Tess grinned at Welch's stunned expression. "Well, somebody's got to look out for you, and obviously Henderson can't watch you all the time. You ate steak last night. You need me, Lanny. Fix that book, and I'll help keep you from becoming the Jesse Helms of Kentucky."

Welch looked dumbfounded.

"I'm your touchstone, Lanny," Tess said. "You said so yourself. We did all right together that summer. And I'm telling you straight on this, that book is too biased. Satire or not, it's mean, Lanny. You've got to fix it."

"No," Welch said, but his voice was thoughtful.

"Come on, Lanny," Tess said. "Think how much fun we can have in politics. And I've learned a lot about schmoozing from Nick. I can be a real asset. You need me. And I'll have plenty of time since I'm not teaching at Decker now. I'll need my afternoons to work at the Foundation, but my weekends are yours."

"Jamieson might have something to say about that," Welch grumped. "And you know damn well you've got the Decker job."

"I think I'd rather be in politics."

"No," Welch said. "God, no. I insist you take the Decker job."

"What about the book?" Tess said, and Welch closed his eyes for a moment in defeat.

"We'll talk about it," he said finally, and Tess leaned forward and kissed him on the cheek.

"I love you, Lanny," she said. "I'm really glad you found me again. And from now on, I'm going to take care of you."

"Oh, God, no," Welch said again.

"CHRISTINE, RENT A CHURCH," Nick said without taking his eyes off Tess as she harangued Welch. "I'm getting married in two weeks."

"It's going to take you longer than that to talk her into it." Christine picked up her steno pad. "Make it six weeks."

"Let's make this expensive." Nick folded his arms and, ignoring Christine, watched Tess argue with Welch. "Might as well make it a big wedding and invite society. Should be good for the firm."

"Tess will want a small wedding." Christine made notes as she spoke. "Out of your house, not a church."

"Fancy caterers," Nick said. "Champagne fountains. The works."

"Tess likes Chinese," Christine said. "Rice wine. Fortune cookies."

"And an orchestra."

"It won't fit in your house. Maybe a classical trio." Christine looked at Tess. "No. Tess would prefer jazz."

Nick watched Tess's rear suddenly curve as she bent to kiss Welch on the cheek. "Order a wedding dress, too. A tight one. No hoopskirts."

"Tess will want to find her own." Christine thought for a moment and made another note. "There's a vintage-clothing store on Twelfth Street."

Nick suddenly transferred his attention back to his secretary. "Did you get all that?" he asked.

"Yes," Christine said serenely. "You can rely on me."

Nick shot her a suspicious glance, but when she gazed back at him without expression, he turned his eyes back to Tess.

"This is going to be a great wedding," he said.

Epilogue

X WEEKS LATER, when the orchestra was finally gone from
ne poolside, Tess wandered through her house in the white
epe wedding dress she'd found at the vintage-clothing store
n Twelfth, sipping champagne and contemplating her fu-
re. She moved through the rooms loving all the color that
ne and Nick had poured into the house over the past weeks
nd yet feeling a little melancholy. She was married now. She
as respectable. Responsible.

She sat on the stairs and looked out at the pristine pool.
ngela climbed into her lap, and she stroked the cat and
ghed.

"Excuse me?" Nick said from behind her, and she turned
see him scowling at her through the stair rails. He was as
eautiful as always, impeccably dressed in his tux, not a hair
it of place. "You just got married," he told her with mock
verity. "You're supposed to be in ecstasy. If you're short on
estasy, I've got a master bedroom you should see."

"I know," Tess said. "I'm the one who painted it yellow."

"I don't mind the yellow," Nick said. "But did you have to
int the ceiling blue and glue on all those glow-in-the-dark
ars? I turned the lights off last night and almost had a cor-
nary when I rolled over."

"Well, I figured I'd be spending a lot of time up there star-
g at it," Tess said. "You know, on my back with the lights
it."

"I know there's a message here I'm not getting," Nick said.

"Now that I'm Mrs. Jekyll, I have to behave. Gina read m
the riot act on this, and she's right. No more risky sex."

Nick started to laugh and then smothered it when he sav
she was serious. "So now you're planning on spending the res
of your life in the missionary position?" His grin brok
through again.

"Hey," Tess said. "I'm adapting. Give me a little credit."

"I'd rather give you a wedding present." Nick came aroun
to the front of the stairs, took her hand and hauled her to he
feet, dumping Angela to the floor in the process. "It's in th
dining room."

"The dining room's empty. We sold the table, rememben
And then you refused to buy the red one I liked, so . . ." Sh
followed him around the bottom of the stairs and the
stopped, stunned.

The dining room was filled with the biggest grand pian
she'd ever seen. And it was bright red.

Nick leaned against it. "I found it in a thrift shop, beliex
it or not."

Tess walked toward it, her smile growing wider by th
minute. "I don't believe it."

"Well, it was black when I found it," Nick said. "I had
painted red. Like it?"

Tess stroked the lacquered red top as she slowly circled th
piano. "I love it. Does it play the Minute Waltz?"

"Not unless you press the right keys," Nick said. "This is
people piano."

"I don't play the piano," Tess said.

"Neither do I."

Tess stopped and looked back at him. "Then what are v
going to do with a dining room full of a piano that neither o
of us can play?"

"I was hoping you'd ask that." Nick loosened his tie. "Le
strike a blow for humanity."